"Feeling better?" Reese asked.

Sadie nodded, then glanced at the grass-covered mound. "Even after all these years, it's hard to believe he's really dead. I've never known anyone so totally alive."

Reese gave her shoulder a squeeze. "That's our Jerry Don. Beside him, everyone else looked like a feeble imitation of life."

"Not you, Reese," Sadie protested.

"You can't fool someone who knows you as well as I do, Sadie. Jerry Don and I weren't even in the same league where you were concerned."

"That's not true. You know you were always my best friend. Besides, you and Jerry Don were a lot alike, always competing in sports, trying to outdo each other. I never think of one of you without thinking of the other."

"Maybe that's part of the problem, Sadie."

Sadie glanced up to find Reese's eyes turned glacier cold. "I don't understand what you're talking about," she said, feeling a strange tightening in her throat.

"I don't suppose you do. You won't let yourself."

Dear Reader,

With her latest novel (of more than fifty!) on the stands this month, award-winning **Nora Roberts** shares her thoughts about Silhouette **Special Edition**:

"I still remember very clearly the feeling I experienced when I sold my first Silhouette **Special Edition**: absolute delight! The **Special Edition** line gave many writers like me an opportunity to grow with the romance genre. These books are indeed special because they allow us to create characters much like ourselves, people we can understand and root for. They are stories of love and hope and commitment. To me, that *is* romance."

Characters you can understand and root for, women and men who share your values, dream your dreams and tap deep inner sources of love and hope—they're a Silhouette **Special Edition** mainstay for six soul-satisfying romances each month. But do other elements—glamorous, faraway settings, intricate, flamboyant plots—sway your reading selections? This month's Silhouette **Special Edition** authors—Nora Roberts, Tracy Sinclair, Kate Meriwether, Pat Warren, Pamela Toth and Laurey Bright—will take you from Arizona to Australia and to points in between, sharing adventures (and misadventures!) of the heart along the way. We hope you'll savor all six novels.

Be like Nora Roberts—share your thoughts about Silhouette **Special Edition**. We welcome your comments.

Warmest wishes,

Leslie Kazanjian, Senior Editor
Silhouette Books
300 East 42nd Street
New York, N.Y. 10017

KATE MERIWETHER
Small-Town Secrets

Silhouette Special Edition

Published by Silhouette Books New York

America's Publisher of Contemporary Romance

SILHOUETTE BOOKS
300 East 42nd St., New York, N.Y. 10017

Copyright © 1989 by Patricia Ahearn

ISBN: 0-373-09513-9

First Silhouette Books printing March 1989

Printed in the U.S.A.

KATE MERIWETHER

is a practicing attorney and lives in Texas. Since she was a young girl, she has loved reading romances, and it was her lifetime dream to write romances that other readers would enjoy.

She was born in the Texas panhandle, a land so recently wrested from the frontier that her great-grandparents were among the first settlers when they arrived in a covered wagon in 1888. The stark beauty of the panhandle, with its sweeping prairies, unending skies and diamond-studded stars, is the romantic setting for *Small-Town Secrets*.

OKLAHOMA

NEW
MEXICO

Amarillo

Tulia

Tascosa

Lubbock

TEXAS

Austin

MEXICO

Gulf of Mexico

N

Underlined places are fictitious

Prologue

Sadie McClure lifted her arms high above her head while her mother helped her ease into the sequined taffeta prom dress.

"Suck in your breath, dear, so I can zip you up."

Sadie took a deep breath and adjusted the bodice across her softly swelling breasts. She'd never before worn a style quite so provocatively bare. She felt sexy and dangerous and grown-up.

Mrs. McClure finished with the back zipper and turned her attention to the front of Sadie's dress. She brought Sadie back to earth with a thud. "Sadie, pull up that bodice. You know your father won't let you leave the house looking like that."

"Oh, Mom, it's senior prom night. Everybody is wearing a strapless dress. Wynona's dress is cut lower than this."

"I've seen Wynona's dress, and it's perfectly modest. Besides, she doesn't have quite as much to fill the top of hers as you do."

Mrs. McClure's chin squared, and Sadie knew she might as well give in. She'd never get past her parents with all this exposed cleavage, and there was no sense ruining the biggest event of her life with a family quarrel. She'd wait until she got to the high school and then adjust her bodice as low as she dared. She gave her mother a mischievous smile. "Okay, Mom. You win." She edged the ivory taffeta high enough for respectability.

"That's much better, dear. You look quite lovely."

Sadie spun around the room in a whirl of swishing taffeta. "I love the sound this dress makes when I move," she exclaimed. "It makes me feel so glamorous and sophisticated."

"I'm sure you're the most sophisticated eighteen-year-old girl in Tascosa, Texas," her mother answered with a droll smile.

Sadie giggled. There were twenty-two girls in her graduating class, and they were all as naive as newborn colts. They talked incessantly about worldly sophistication, they lusted for sensual experience with the eager zest of the uninitiated; but in a rural community inhabited by fewer than five hundred people, they couldn't make a move without their parents knowing. Before breakfast time tomorrow, Sadie's mother and father would discover that she'd shocked the whole school with her daring décolletage. But by then it would be too late, Sadie thought with gleeful pleasure. The deed would be done.

There was a knock on Sadie's bedroom door. "Sadie, the boys are here," called her father.

"I'll be out in just a minute," she answered, rushing to the mirror to see if her hair or makeup needed any last-minute adjustments. "Is my hair *really* okay like this?" she asked, suddenly nervous that the new style, swept back on the sides with pearl-studded clips, might be all wrong with her dress.

Mrs. McClure came to stand beside Sadie at the mirror. "You look like a princess," she said softly.

Their glances met in the mirrored reflection. Tears of happiness welled in Sadie's eyes. "Thanks, Mom." She gave her mother a warm hug. "I guess I'm the luckiest girl in the world."

There was a second, impatient knock, followed by a different male voice. "Sadie, we're waiting on you. Let's go to the prom."

"You'd better go, Sadie. You don't want to keep Prince Charming waiting."

Sadie threw open the door to her sweetheart and his best friend. Jerry Don Wallace, blond, handsome, and outgoing, stood there with Reese Chandler, dark, equally handsome, and brooding.

"Wow!" said both boys simultaneously.

Jerry Don whistled. "Wow!" he said again. "I guess it was worth the wait." His gaze traveled up and down Sadie's ivory taffeta dress, then to her bare neck and shoulders and the reddish-gold hair that hung in loose waves down her back, and finally lingered on her pretty face.

"You guys don't look so bad yourselves," she answered with a dazzling smile. In their rented tuxedos they looked like men, not boys, with muscles born of ranch work and athletics straining against the confines of formal wear.

Mr. McClure joined the group and stretched out his arms to Sadie. "You look mighty pretty," he said with fatherly pride. "Mother, get your camera and take a picture for the family album."

Jerry Don grinned, and Sadie blushed. At every event in Sadie's life, Mrs. McClure took photographs. Jerry Don loved clowning for the camera and relished each opportunity, while Sadie always felt a little embarrassed by all the attention. But tonight she was glad for the snapshot session. This was the happiest night of her life, and she wanted a photograph to remind her.

For not only was this the night of the senior prom; it was also the night when she and Jerry Don would become engaged. They'd talked about it for weeks and kept it a secret from everyone but Reese. Tonight they'd announce it to the rest of the world, and Jerry Don would give her an engagement ring with a tiny diamond. They'd have to wait until they finished college to get married, of course. But four years would fly past, and then they'd have a big wedding and settle down and raise a family. They both wanted to have at least three kids. They were going to have a wonderful life together, and tonight was only the beginning!

Mrs. McClure returned with her camera and gave quick instructions. "Sadie, let me get a picture of the three of you. Reese, you get on one side of Sadie, and Jerry Don, you get on the other." She held the camera to her eye and tried to focus it. "Hold still, Jerry Don. And please, no tricks this time." The flashbulb popped. "Jerry Don, why did you have to do that?" Mrs. McClure scolded. Just as she'd pressed the button, Jerry Don had leaned down and leered into the bodice of Sadie's dress.

It took several attempts and a muttered warning from Reese before Jerry Don quit his antics and let Mrs. McClure get the snapshot she wanted.

"Now," she said. "Sadie and Jerry Don. The two of you."

Reese stepped aside and watched. Sadie caught his glance and gave him a shy smile. It was a little awkward to leave Reese out. Somehow the three of them belonged together. They'd always been a trio and done everything together since kindergarten. Sadie didn't want the engagement to force Reese out of their lives. This was a problem she hadn't anticipated when she and Jerry Don had been making their marriage plans. There had to be a solution. Maybe Reese would marry

Wynona Taylor, Sadie's best girlfriend, and the four of them could go on the same way they always had.

Sadie didn't want anything to change. She loved Jerry Don, and he was the person she wanted to marry. She loved Reese, too, but in a different way. Besides, Jerry Don needed her to protect him from his little-boy ways. Reese was self-sufficient and mature. He didn't need anything from Sadie or anyone else. But Reese would be good for Wynona, who, like Jerry Don, needed a lot of affection and looking after. In the split second it took for the flashbulb to pop, Sadie had planned a double wedding and a double lifetime of bliss for the four of them.

Her thoughts were interrupted with more directions from her mother. "Sadie, you and Reese, come over here so I can snap your picture."

"Sadie and Reese?" Jerry Don protested. "My girl and my best friend, without me? No way!"

Sadie couldn't tell whether Jerry Don was teasing or not.

"Never mind, Mrs. McClure," Reese said. "I'll get my picture taken with Wynona when we get to her house. She's my date for tonight."

"Good move, Chandler," Jerry Don said. "I always figured if I left you and Sadie alone for one minute, you'd steal her from me." He gave a loud guffaw of laughter. "One last picture," he said to Mrs. McClure. "Me and my best friend, Reese Chandler. Put up your dukes, Chandler." Mrs. McClure took the last photo on the roll of film—a mock boxing scene with Jerry Don and Reese squared off, scowling at each other, fists ready to punch.

"That's it," Jerry Don said with another burst of boisterous laughter. He threw one arm across Reese's shoulder, the other across Sadie's. "Now, let's go to the prom. History is going to be made tonight."

Chapter One

Sadie McClure whipped her yellow sports car off the dirt road and parked it beside a farmhouse surrounded by cottonwood trees. The hot summer sun had beaten down on her for hours, and her long, reddish-gold hair was wind tossed and her back sweat soaked from her long drive. She braced herself against the steering wheel and drew a deep breath. This is Tascosa, she thought. I've come home.

She gazed across the intimidating expanse of Texas prairie and experienced a confusing mixture of awe and dread. The vast open space made her feel small and vulnerable, with no place to hide her fears—or her guilt. I've come home, she repeated, but only because

Mom needs me. And I won't stay a single day longer than I have to.

She reached for a tissue and wiped beads of perspiration from her face. Tilting the rearview mirror, she gave herself a cursory inspection. Her nose was sunburned, and her hair was a mess. No one would mistake her for a high-school cheerleader and beauty queen. But that had been ten years ago....

Sadie's mind wandered. She hadn't intended to come back to Tascosa for her high-school reunion, which was scheduled for the upcoming Fourth of July weekend. She'd settled into her new life in Austin, where there were no painful reminders of betrayal and lost love. Over the past few years, her trips back to Tascosa had become less and less frequent, and Sadie had decided it would be better to skip her class reunion. No sense stirring up memories she'd prefer to forget. She wouldn't be here now, except that her old school chum Wynona Evans had telephoned last night with bad news.

Wynona. She'd been Sadie's friend since elementary school, though they didn't keep in close contact anymore. Six years ago, and much to everyone's surprise, Wynona had married Tom Evans after an almost nonexistent courtship. They now lived with their four kids on a prospering wheat farm and had frequent contact with Sadie's mother, Nelda McClure, who were their closest neighbor. Earlier in the week, when Nelda McClure had tripped over a garden hose and broken her leg, Wynona hadn't wanted to worry

Sadie by reporting the news—until, as Wynona had explained on the telephone last night, it had become obvious that Mrs. McClure wouldn't be able to take care of herself because the heavy plaster cast made it so difficult for her to get around.

"I thought you should know, hon." Wynona's voice had been tinged with doubt whether she'd done the right thing to call Sadie. "I've been trying to run by and check on her, but that's not enough. This afternoon one of the neighbors found her sprawled on the floor with a bump on her head. She needs someone to stay there with her, and what with a new baby and all, I can't do it myself. The doctor says your mom is going to need a week or two to get her strength back."

Sadie had been both concerned and puzzled. "Why didn't Mom call me as soon as it happened?" she asked. "Didn't she know I'd want to come take care of her until she could manage for herself again?"

Wynona had tried to shrug off the problem. "She probably thought it would be too hard for you to get off work."

"She knew I was planning my vacation. Summer is our slack time at work, if there is such a thing."

When Sadie had continued to fret, Wynona had silenced her with a single statement. "Sadie, your mother knows you don't like to come back to Tascosa. She wouldn't ask you to do it for her sake, hon."

"I'll be there tomorrow," Sadie had answered, then hung up the receiver.

Sadie now unbuckled herself from the low-slung front seat and stepped onto the gravel driveway, stretching at the waist and leaning backward to loosen her kinked muscles. She glanced at her watch. Barely two o'clock. She'd made good time once she hit the long, open stretches of the plains. She reached for her purse and keys. The rest of her stuff could wait until later.

She started up the walk toward the wood-shingled house that had been her childhood home. The shutters and trim had a new coat of white paint that looked perky against the charcoal-gray shingles, and a pot of red geraniums brightened the stoop. The house looked as well tended as it had when Sadie's father was alive.

As always, the thought of her father brought a lump to Sadie's throat. He'd been rugged and strong, a sun-bronzed rancher with inexhaustible energy and glowing health. And then suddenly, when Sadie was a junior in college, he'd had a massive heart attack and died before they could get him to the hospital. If he had lived, would things have turned out any differently? Would he have realized that things were going wrong between Sadie and Jerry Don Wallace, her childhood sweetheart? Would he have kept Sadie from making that terrible mistake of breaking their engagement?

Sadie stopped at the top step and gripped the porch railing. Waves of regret washed over her, but she choked back the sob in her throat. No! Don't do this to yourself. It's over, all of it. Daddy's dead. Jerry

Don is dead. And nobody can change what's happened. She drew a deep, shuddering breath and forced her lips into a bright smile to greet her mother.

"Mom," she called. "Mom, I'm home."

She closed the screen door behind her and hurried through the familiar rooms. The fresh scent of lemon and furniture wax tugged at her senses. Everything was just the same, she thought, noticing the way the afternoon sun filtered through the sheer priscilla curtains. From almost forgotten habit, she dropped her purse and car keys on the dining-room table.

"Mom, can you hear me? I'm home," she said, feeling another lump form in her throat as she reached her mother's bedroom at the back of the house.

Nelda McClure tried to sit up in bed. "Oh, Sadie," she cried in a small, relieved voice, stretching out her arms. "How did you know?"

Sadie sat down on the edge of the bed and buried her face against her mother's shoulder. When she was a child, she had turned to her mother in exactly this way for comfort and reassurance. Now the shoulder that used to be so firm and strong against her cheek was frail and bony. Now it was the mother who needed comfort and reassurance from the daughter. Sadie wished there were some way to ease the tightness in her throat that made it so hard for her to speak.

"Wynona called me," she said, searching her mother's face and finding age lines that hadn't been there before, and a gray, pasty color that was new. "Mom, you should've called me yourself. You know

I would've come right away if you'd told me about your broken leg.''

Nelda shook her head. "I didn't want you to know. I really thought I'd be able to manage by myself. Remember that time you broke your leg skiing at Santa Fe, and the way you whizzed around on your crutches? I figured I'd be able to do the same thing."

The women exchanged rueful glances. "Mom, I was sixteen years old then. Nothing can slow you down at that age."

"Guess I should've thought about that sooner." Nelda rubbed a sore place under her arm. "I could use a teenager's firm muscle for this spot where the crutches rub."

Sadie forced her lips into a jaunty smile, wondering whether her mother would see through her pretense. "You're all I've got, Mom, and I'm all you've got. When you need someone, I want to be here with you." Sadie's fingers made restless folds in the crumpled bedsheets.

Nelda stilled Sadie's hand with a grip that was surprisingly strong. "Thanks for coming, Sadie. None of the neighbors could stay with me at this time of year— not with the wheat ready to be harvested. Everybody's too busy."

Sadie returned the pressure of her mother's fingers, then reached to give her a hug. "You don't have to explain," she whispered. "I'm glad I could come." It was only a little white lie, and in some ways it was true. It was always hard for Sadie to come back home to Tascosa, because the past closed in and suffocated her with painful memories. Yet this time it somehow seemed right to be here. Her mother was frightened by the unexpected weakness of her body. Maybe Sadie's physical strength and vitality would be reassuring to her.

Sadie picked up the various prescription bottles on the bedside stand and read the instructions. There was an empty water glass, and a basin of soap-scummed water with a soiled washcloth, as though her mother had attempted a spit bath. "Let me get some fresh water and help you bathe," Sadie said. "Then I'll change these sheets and find something for you to eat. While I'm working, I want you to tell me every word the doctor said to you."

"Welcome home, Sadie," her mother said, finding the strength to chuckle. "I'd forgotten how much I missed your bossiness." Nelda leaned forward and let Sadie plump her pillows.

Sadie smoothed back her mother's hair and suddenly noticed that it was no longer a bright, reddish-gold like her own but was instead a dull, dusty, peach color. When had her mother's hair started to turn gray? Was it when Sadie's father died, or was it later, after Sadie had left home? She couldn't remember. She'd been so wrapped up in herself and being in love with Jerry Don that she hadn't paid any attention.

"Am I being bossy?" she asked, putting aside her musings. "I'm just trying to get you well as soon as possible so I can get back to the important business of running the schools of the great state of Texas. The teachers monitor the students, the principals monitor the teachers, the superintendents monitor the principals, and the state accreditation team monitors everybody."

"Is *monitor* another word for *boss*, my bossy daughter?"

Sadie and her mother exchanged a smile. It was best, for now, to put aside their anxious fears for each other and strive for normalcy, Sadie thought. She began a vivacious, nonstop rendition of her life in the state capital, Austin, while she worked with seemingly perpetual energy to straighten the bedroom and refresh her mother's sagging spirits. By the time Sadie had finished the bath and changed the sheets, Nelda was exhausted and ready for a nap.

"You've worn me out," Nelda scolded gently. "I'm not used to all this exertion."

"Rest, then, while I take a shower and clean up. Later on I'll see what I can find for you to eat. You'll be hungry when you wake up."

"Someone from the church sent over some chicken broth," Nelda said. "I think Reese put it in the freezer."

Sadie whirled. "Reese Chandler?" The name carried all the impact of a physical blow. Reese had been Jerry Don's best friend since childhood—and Sadie's best friend, too, most of the time. But he was also part of the reason for her never-ending guilt. She wasn't ready to deal with her unresolved relationship with Reese Chandler. "Has he been here?"

"Of course," Nelda answered, her face puzzled. "He comes by almost every day, to check the wheat and see if it's ready to harvest. Reese still leases the farm from me, Sadie."

"Oh, sure. I'd forgotten." Sadie tucked the sheets around her mother's thin shape and slipped from the room before Nelda could say anything else. "I'll be in my room," Sadie called from the hallway. "Let me know if you need anything."

Sadie paused at the paneled wood door of her old bedroom, shifting her luggage and hesitating as she reached for the doorknob. When she turned it and stepped inside, she'd be walking straight into her past. She wasn't sure she wanted to do that. Then she shrugged. What other choice did she have? She twisted the handle and threw open the door.

There were white-with-purple eyelet embroidery ruffles everywhere—on the bed, at the windows, around the dressing table. The purple-and-white streamers of her cheerleader pom-poms were still tacked to the bulletin board. The room was a cheerleader's ruffled shrine, decorated in the official colors of her high school. Everything was exactly as it had been when she was a teenager, Sadie thought uneasily as she stepped inside. Why hadn't her mother packed this stuff in boxes and stored it in the attic, where it belonged? There were plenty of ghosts to haunt their memories without harboring this one.

Sadie set down her suitcases and walked slowly to the bulletin board. Old high-school pictures were still there: Sadie and Wynona in their purple-and-white cheerleader outfits, waving their pom-poms; Sadie in her white graduation cap and gown, with the purple cord that marked her as an honors graduate.

Her eyes stayed on the safe pictures: Sadie trying on her prom formal, her mother kneeling on the floor to mark the hem; Sadie astride the quarter horse Daddy had given her for one birthday; Sadie with Jerry Don and Reese on the night of the senior prom; Sadie perched high on the windmill, waving her cowboy hat at fluffy white clouds.

There were no more safe pictures. Yet Sadie couldn't seem to stop gazing at the photos while her heart looked back in time. She reached to unfasten the photo of herself with Jerry Don and Reese stretched across the hood of Jerry Don's new car. All three of them were grinning: Jerry Don, so full of life then, blond and blue-eyed, handsome as they come and just as devil-may-care. In the photo he had one arm around Sadie's waist while he smiled adoringly into the camera, a dimple twinkling at the corner of his lips. Sadie was snuggled against him, her lips parted in a smile of sheer exuberance, with one hand linked to Reese's. Reese, a little apart, leaned toward Sadie, his cheek against her hair. Well, Sadie thought, Mom's camera certainly caught that perfect moment in our inseparable trio. It had been Jerry Don's twenty-first birthday, the year he'd gotten the silver-blue Thunderbird—

Sadie dropped the picture as though it had burned her fingers. Jerry Don had been so proud of his new car that bright and happy day. Nobody had dreamed that a year later he'd be dead. How could they have been so young and foolish? she wondered. Did they think the fun and games would go on forever, that they'd laugh their way through life and never know any heartache? She looked at the photo again.

Maybe Reese had known, she conceded. There had been a melancholy expression in his eyes, though she hadn't been aware of it at the time. If Reese had suspected they wouldn't all live happily ever after, he hadn't bothered to tell them.

A strange sense of anger rushed through Sadie— anger at Reese, anger at herself, anger at life in general. What glorious hopes they'd had then. But look how things had turned out: Jerry Don had died, with his Thunderbird wrapped around a tree; Reese had become a lonely rancher following a hasty marriage and divorce; and Sadie was still trying to run away from a guilt-scarred past.

Sadie jerked off her clothes and marched into the adjoining bathroom. With the shower going full blast, she shed new tears for Jerry Don and the sweetness of their first love. When she emerged, she blew her nose, dried her eyes, and put on fresh lipstick. By the time she was dressed and went outside to air-dry her hair in the sunshine, her trademark smile was back in place and there was a new resolution that put fresh starch in her backbone. She was twenty-eight now, and a woman. It was high time for her to face the future. Six years was long enough to grieve over the past.

Sadie made her way to a grove of cottonwood trees in the backyard and sat down on the swing her father had made for her when she was a little girl. She brushed her hair, welcoming the prairie breeze that quickly dried her long tresses. On impulse, she bent her knees and leaned forward to thrust the swing into motion, gliding toward the sky, then falling back in the direction of the tall green grass. A laugh bubbled up from deep inside her. How she'd always loved this tree swing! Jerry Don and Reese used to take turns pushing her higher and faster, trying without success to frighten her. She could almost hear their bantering laughter in her mind, and her own unfailing response: "Higher, you guys, higher!"

Filled with some deep, remembered joy, Sadie cried, "Here I go, over the top!"

She kicked her feet and surged forward, then jumped from the swing when it reached its zenith and flung herself lightly onto the soft grass below. Laughing, she fell onto her back and stretched out her arms, grabbing snatches of grass in either hand while she stared up at the azure sky filled with golden-lined white clouds.

"Sadie, are you okay?" came a shout, and there was the sound of footsteps pounding across the yard.

She lifted herself on one elbow and turned. It had to be Reese. There was no other voice on earth like his—a deep, rich baritone. Before she lifted her face to look at him, she tried to brace herself. She hadn't had sufficient time to prepare for this moment, yet suddenly it was upon her. She wasn't sure how to respond. They saw each other so seldom that there was always a certain tension between them, marked by a strange blend of emotions that was half pleasure and half pain.

Reese Chandler dropped onto one knee beside Sadie, his voice conveying nothing more than the casual, brotherly concern he'd always shown with her misadventures. "Did you hurt yourself?" he asked. "I saw you fall off the swing." In a reflex motion, his hand shot out to grip her shoulder.

She lifted her eyes. Reese's dark brown hair was a little longer at the nape of his neck, but still had the same loose wave that he always tried to brush away. His scent was the same: clean and male, permeated with an indescribable aura of sunshine and earth, growing crops and animals—things that were vital and alive. There was a stubble of dark beard, as though he hadn't shaved for a day or two. His ears were the same—well formed and tight against his head; his jaw still square; his nose with the same interesting crook at the bridge. His fingers dug into her shoulder, and she felt the same strength in his grip, combined with the same gentleness.

Their eyes met, and Sadie quickly glanced away. She'd forgotten his eyes were that shade of blue-gray; forgotten how he could look at her with that kind of intensity. His eyes were like this prairie: they didn't leave you any place to hide.

"I didn't fall," Sadie said, edging her shoulder away from the warmth of his fingers, trying to ignore the sudden rush of her response. "I jumped."

Reese frowned at her as his tone turned angry. "That was a stupid thing to do. You could've broken your ankle. Then we'd have two patients to take care of, and we don't even have time to take care of one."

Sadie's hazel eyes flew downward to hide her reaction to him. How could this be happening? She'd just gotten here and already she and Reese were having an argument. Hadn't anything at all changed between them, not even after six years? Was anger still the only way they could communicate? Anger was a familiar part of their relationship, a chronic barrier that kept them at a safe emotional distance from each other.

And it hadn't been half an hour since she'd promised herself that she was going to bury the dead past, Sadie thought, feeling irritated with Reese for bringing out the same old childish reactions in her. She sat up cross-legged in the grass and glared at him. "Thank you for such a warm welcome," she said. "I'm glad we can pick up exactly where we left off, with a typically stupid argument. Now I know for sure I'm really home."

A tense muscle twitched at the corner of Reese's jaw, and the expression on his face became guarded. He let out a slow sigh and sat down on the grass beside Sadie. "I'm sorry," he said. "I didn't know you were here until I saw that yellow convertible in the driveway and figured it had to be yours. I came around the corner of the house, looking for you, and saw you go flying through the air. It scared the hell out of me."

Sadie's lips trembled. It was always this way. First he made her mad, then he made her feel guilty. Reese had been her best friend ever since she could remember, but it was the stormiest friendship she'd ever known. They were perpetually fighting about something, and it didn't much seem to matter what it was. With Jerry Don she'd experienced affection and playfulness. It wasn't that way with Reese, though. Reese might be the one she could count on when the chips were down, but the rest of the time their relationship consisted of bickering and confusion. If Jerry Don had been Sadie's sunshine, Reese had been her thunderstorm. And as usual, Reese made it seem as though the cloudburst were all her fault.

They couldn't start out fighting again, Sadie told herself. She needed to do something to set things right. She managed a bright smile and forced a time-out signal with her hands. "Why don't we practice this play from the beginning?" she said. "Let's start over.

I'm at the swing. You're at the driveway. Okay?'' She gave a sharp whistle to start the new play, the way coach used to do at football practice.

Reese grinned, a little abashed. "Welcome home, Sadie." He started to offer his hand for a handshake, then with some awkwardness leaned forward to give Sadie a hug. His arms were around her, his chest solid against her cheek, but their bodies made contact for only an instant before he started to pull away from her.

Why were they still so awkward about touching each other? Sadie suddenly realized that Reese didn't know how to handle this greeting any better than she did. She lifted herself onto her knees and leaned against Reese, tilting her face toward his before he could move farther away. "Aren't you going to give me a kiss?"

She could see the Adam's apple work in his throat. Did Reese feel the same guilt Sadie felt when they touched, or had he forgotten that terrible day six years ago? She remembered the chaste, childish kisses they'd exchanged in prior years. Only once had they kissed in a way that—

Sadie's eyes opened wide in surprised remembrance and found Reese giving her a strange, twisted smile, as though he, too, were thinking of another time, another kiss. His arms, which had almost let go of her, tightened.

"Reese, I didn't mean—" she murmured, but her protest was silenced by the urgent pressure of his mouth against hers. The stubble of his beard was rough against the tender skin of her chin, yet it was somehow erotic rather than unpleasant. Reese held the kiss until Sadie's fiercely pounding heart caused a roaring in her ears as loud as any tornado that had ever ripped across the prairie. Instinctively her arms wound upward and twined around his neck, and she felt her heart hammering underneath her thin blouse. A sigh formed at the base of her throat, and she heard Reese groan as he pulled her close and hard against him. The kiss deepened, and with it the pressure of his body against hers as his hand moved up from her waist.

An alarm shrilled inside Sadie's spinning brain. Watch out, Sadie. This is happening too fast, it warned. You're not ready for this. Not yet. Not with Reese. Reluctantly Sadie fought her way back from aroused desire. "No, Reese," she whispered. "Don't rush things. I'm too confused."

Muttering an oath, Reese pulled away and let his arms fall to his sides.

Sadie averted her eyes and tore feebly at clumps of grass. If only her heart would quit pounding so hard! She was sure Reese could see how much their kiss had affected her, just as she could see how he was struggling to regain control. Would he be angry with her again? Or would he realize, as she did, that they couldn't let this sudden, overpowering physical attraction keep them from resolving the deeper problems of their relationship? She tossed a handful of grass into the air and waited for him to break the silence.

"We aren't kids anymore, Sadie," Reese said in a strained, husky voice. "We're adults, with feelings that can get out of hand." He gave her that intense gaze that bored into her very soul, then swore under his breath and looked away. "Why did you have to come back, Sadie? Why didn't you just stay in Austin, where you belong?"

Chapter Two

Reese's harsh words were almost like a physical blow. Sadie averted her head and stared toward the house. There were blue morning glories in full bloom climbing a lattice at the back gate, and near the kitchen door were rosebushes loaded with yellow buds and blossoms. From vines behind her came the sweet fragrance of honeysuckle, and from the cottonwood boughs overhead came the cheerful trill of a mockingbird. The details tugged at her consciousness, reminding her that the physical place of her childhood would always be her emotional home, no matter how hard she tried to run away.

"Are you telling me I don't belong in Tascosa?" she asked in a defiant voice, squaring her chin. "That's odd. I didn't know I'd lose my citizenship if I didn't come home more often than once or twice a year." Sadie brushed blades of grass from her shorts and legs, then stood. "I'll go down to the courthouse in the morning and be sure the property taxes are paid."

"Stop it." Reese remained sitting in a loose coil and let Sadie look down at him, as though he wanted her to know he wasn't intimidated by having her tower above him. His voice was as icy as her own. "Stop acting like a spoiled child."

"You're a fine one to talk."

"Look, Sadie, everything was going just fine without you. Your mother had gotten used to living alone, with you breezing in for a day or two when you got to feeling guilty about her. What do you think it's going to do to her when you leave this time, after she's started to depend on you, instead of the neighbors?"

Sadie's fingers worked at the furrowed ridge that formed between her eyebrows when she frowned. "I guess we'll deal with that when the times comes. Right now it's pretty obvious that she needs me for a week or two."

"We could've managed without you."

Sadie's arms folded across her chest in the way she characteristically showed her indignation. Who was Reese to question her right to be here? "I'm her only child, and I want to be with her. Besides that, Wynona told me Mom had stumbled with her crutches yesterday and one of the neighbors found her on the floor."

Reese uncoiled himself and rose with the fluid ease of a rattlesnake about to strike. "Who in the hell do you think found her, Sadie?"

Sadie's hand flew to her mouth in surprise. "You!" She felt heat rise in her cheeks and knew she was blushing. "Oh, Reese, I'm sorry. I should've realized you'd been trying to take care of Mom yourself." She reached out to touch his arm and felt the hardened muscle under his blue plaid shirt. "I do appreciate everything you've done, Reese." She gave him a tremulous smile.

He shoved his hands into the pockets of his faded jeans and let out his breath in a soft sigh. "Come to think of it, I'm glad you're here to take over," he admitted. "It's pretty hard for a guy to take care of... well, you know, the things a woman needs." There was a shyness in his expression that made him suddenly look much younger than his twenty-eight years and more like the teenage boy who'd spent more time at Sadie's house than he did at his own. "Your mom was always like a second mother to me," he added.

"And you were like the son she always wanted," Sadie replied, for the first time giving Reese a genuine smile. "Mom always preferred you to Jerry Don. Of course, you never broke her china lamp or knocked out windows with a baseball bat the way he did."

They both tried to laugh. The painful name had been spoken aloud. *Jerry Don.* Maybe things would get easier now that Sadie had conjured forth the ghost that haunted them both.

There was the sound of a car door slamming, followed by the sound of children running. "Aaron, just a minute! I'm trying to get the baby!"

Sadie and Reese exchanged glances. "That must be Wynona," Sadie said, hurrying toward the driveway at the front of the house. "Oh, how wonderful! I haven't seen her new baby yet."

Reese lingered behind while Sadie and Wynona flung themselves into each other's arms, Wynona's baby more or less wrapped in the same hug of greeting.

"What a beautiful baby!" Sadie said, smiling down at the infant. "So you're little Melanie," she crooned, stroking the baby's cheek.

There was a tug at the cuff of Sadie's shorts.

"I'm Becka," said a little girl with short blond curls. "I'm four."

"Yes, I remember you," Sadie said, leaning down to give the child a hug. "My goodness, you've gotten to be such a big girl!"

Becka pointed toward another towheaded child running down the driveway. "That's Biff. He's my twin brother."

"I'm Aaron," said the eldest child, extending his hand in manly fashion. "I'm five, going on six."

Sadie gave her oldest and dearest girlfriend a warm smile. "They've all got your blond hair and blue eyes, Wynona."

"Yes, even though Tom says his brown hair and brown eyes were supposed to be dominant. He did a genetic chart like he does with our registered cattle, but somehow our genes have flunked the science test." While she talked, Wynona's eyes stayed busy, watching the children, and occasionally she called out to one of them with maternal instructions. When she caught sight of Reese, she gave him a calculating look, then turned back to Sadie. "Reese must've been surprised to find you here," she said.

Sadie tried to deflect her friend's curiosity. She didn't want Wynona to start probing the details of their meeting, not while her lips still tingled from the pressure of Reese's mouth. "I don't think he was as surprised as Mom was."

"How is your mother doing today?" Wynona asked. "I brought a fresh peach cobbler for your supper, just in case she feels like eating something."

"She seems okay—just tired and sort of depressed that she can't manage her crutches the way a teenager would. I need to go check on her and see if she's finished her nap. She was snoring like a baby when I went down to the tree swing." Sadie started toward the front door while Wynona began to gather her chicks like a mother hen. "Come on in with us, Reese, and I'll make some iced tea."

"Can't do it," he said. "I've got to get back over to the other place and check the wheat."

"Tom says our section will be ready for the combine tomorrow," Wynona said. "I hope it doesn't rain until we get our wheat harvested."

"I'm betting it won't rain until the Fourth of July."

Wynona laughed. "That should be a safe bet. Doesn't it usually rain on the Fourth of July?"

Sadie felt left out. When Daddy was alive, rain and crops had been the constant topic of family conversation, but that was long ago. In Austin, Sadie gave her thought and effort to other things, and she'd forgotten that farmers and ranchers were totally dependent upon nature. They made their living from the land, and they had to stay in close harmony with it. Only the vigilant could survive.

Becka's chubby hand reached up to take Sadie's. "Would you help me get the box of toys from Aunt Nelda's closet?" asked Becka. "She always lets us play with them when we come to see her."

Wynona shifted the baby onto her shoulder. "I guess you didn't know your mother gave up on you to provide her with grandchildren and unofficially adopted my brood. Come on, kids, let's get the toy box so you can play *quietly* while I visit with the grown-ups."

Reese started down the driveway to his navy-and-silver pickup truck. He was moving fast now, needing to make up the time he'd lost from his ranch duties.

"Aren't you going to stay and have a bite of my peach cobbler?" Wynona called after him.

He turned long enough to give her a friendly wave. "Not now. I don't have time. Save me some for later." He climbed into the truck, and its powerful engine roared when he pumped the accelerator. He honked goodbye at the crossroads and was gone in a cloud of dust.

Sadie found her mother sitting upright in bed, thumbing through a magazine. Already Nelda Mc-Clure's color was better, and she seemed more comfortable.

"Surprise," Sadie said, stepping into the bedroom. "We have company."

"I heard the children." Nelda spread her arms and embraced each of Wynona's children in turn, then released them to go and play with their toys. "Sadie, I'd like to get out of bed for a while. Will you help me to the bathroom, dear?"

Nelda's steps were clumsy, and she leaned heavily against Sadie's shoulder rather than use the crutches. The effort of getting up seemed to exhaust her, but rather than complain, Nelda congratulated herself that this time she hadn't tripped and fallen. After she finished in the bathroom, she insisted on sitting in an armchair with her leg propped up while they visited.

Wynona sat in a rocker so she could nurse the baby, and Sadie stretched across the end of the bed. There was neighborhood gossip to relate, most of it having to do with which fields were ready for harvest and which farmers had managed well and would have good crops.

Sadie rolled over onto her back to listen. The conversation was a lifetime away from her own current experiences, and she had nothing to contribute. Had she lived in the city so long that she'd never fit in again?

"Sadie, I'm sorry. We must be boring you out of your mind," Wynona said when she realized that Sadie's eyes were closed.

"No, no, I'm just tired. I got up early to pack and was on the road at six o'clock. It's a long drive from Austin to Tascosa, especially with the hot sun beating down." Sadie hoped her excuse was convincing. She hadn't meant to be rude.

"Everything in Tascosa goes on pretty much the same," Wynona said. "We follow the seasons just like we've always done. About the only thing that changes is a new grave or a new baby."

Sadie reflected on Wynona's comment. Yes, that was part of what was wonderful about Tascosa—and about rural life in general. The continuity, the order, the sense of permanence. Roots, that's what it was. Good, solid roots, sunk deep into the earth. It had been only three years since Sadie had moved to Austin, yet the growing, prosperous city had already changed more than Tascosa had in Sadie's entire lifetime.

"Tell us about your job," Wynona insisted. "I know you've said you work on a monitoring team, but what does that mean?"

"The agency where I work oversees all the public schools in the state," Sadie explained. "We have to be sure the required curriculum is being properly taught by teachers who are properly certified. There's more to it than that, of course, but that's it in a nutshell."

Sadie turned to Wynona and tried to fathom how much she really wanted to know and how much was merely polite inquiry. "We go out in teams and check to be sure the schools meet accreditation standards."

"You mean you go to different towns and different schools?" Wynona turned the baby across her knees and burped her.

"Yes. I'm on the road three or four nights a week."

"Is it exciting, or do you get tired of it?" Wynona smiled down at her sleeping baby. "If I'm away from home one or two nights a *year*, it's a big deal. I was gone three nights when I was in the hospital having Melanie."

Sadie sighed. "I like being on the move and meeting lots of new people, but sometimes I just want to curl up in my own bed instead of waking up in another motel and trying to figure out which town I'm in."

Nelda McClure glanced at her daughter with a troubled expression. "I thought you were happy, Sadie."

"Oh, I *am* happy, Mom. You know me. I thrive on the stimulation. Once a cheerleader, always a cheerleader."

"It's no wonder you've never gotten married," her mother replied. "You don't stay in one town long enough to meet anybody."

"Oh, I meet lots of men, Mom." Sadie gave her mother a mischievous grin. "I daresay I've met almost every eligible man in the Lone Star state. I've probably covered every mile of it at least twice."

Nelda gave her attention to the baby sleeping on Wynona's lap. She said nothing more, but her thoughts were obvious: it was time for Sadie to settle down and have a family, as Wynona had done.

"Sadie isn't like me," Wynona said softly. "What I wanted was a husband and children, and I got the best there was of both. There's not a better man anywhere than my Tom, and the kids are healthy and happy and lots of fun, even if they run me ragged sometimes. They're all I need and all I want." Wynona leaned her head against the back of the chair and let it rock gently. "But Sadie's different. She always was. She wanted to push herself in every way she could, and compete, and develop her talents. She's looked inside herself for her strength, instead of finding strength in things that are outside her, the way I did." Wynona reached over to squeeze Sadie's hand. "I think the good Lord meant to make all different kinds of people, and it doesn't mean someone like

Sadie is peculiar or less of a woman. I say more power to you, hon.''

Sadie reached for a tissue from the box on the nightstand. Wynona's stout defense had touched her, and tears filled Sadie's eyes. She'd had no idea Wynona was so perceptive. Sadie blew her nose. "Thanks, friend," she said softly. "I needed that. You have no idea how many nights I've lain awake wondering what's the matter with me that I want to have a career *and* a family.''

"You're special, Sadie. It's going to take a special man for you, that's all." Wynona pushed her blond curls away from her face. "Look at you. It's been ten years since we graduated from high school, and you've gotten more beautiful. Here I am, plump around the middle because I can't lose the weight I gained with the baby, and your waist is slimmer now than it was then. If you weren't my best friend and the sweetest person I know, I'd probably hate you for being so gorgeous!''

There was the sound of racing feet, and Becka burst into the room. "Mommy, make Biff give me the ball. It's my turn!''

Biff was right behind her. "No, Mommy, she had it first, and she kept it and kept it. Now it's my turn!''

Awakened by the twins, the baby squirmed and began to make noises.

Wynona got to her feet. "My rest period is over. Back to being a drill sergeant." She checked the baby's diaper, then shifted her into the crook of one elbow.

"Go put the toys back in the box," she told the twins. "We've got to go home and cook supper for your daddy." Somehow Wynona held the baby in one arm and used the other to round up the remaining children, saw that the toys were neatly put away, and got everybody into the car and seat-belted. "See you later, hon," she said to Sadie in the driveway, giving her a cheerful wave. "Be sure to save some of my peach cobbler for Reese. It's his favorite dessert, and if I know him, he'll come back for it after he's finished in the fields."

The slender arc of the moon had drifted midway across the horizon when Sadie stepped onto the front porch. For a moment it seemed that she'd stepped into an unending velvet darkness. When her eyes adjusted, she could see faint moon-beamed outlines of the nearby cottonwood trees, the flickering mercury-vapor light from a neighbor's barn some quarter of a mile away. She'd forgotten how dark it was out in the country, away from everything.

Sadie sat down on the porch steps and gazed up into the sky. Was there anyplace else on earth where the stars twinkled so brightly? she wondered. When she had been a young teenager, she and Jerry Don and Reese used to stretch out on the grass and watch the constellations parade across the night sky. They'd taken turns telling ghost stories, trying to scare each other to death.

A wistful smile toyed at the corners of Sadie's lips. We were all so happy then, she thought. Why did everything have to go wrong?

She sighed. This was the question she had never permitted herself to ask, because there was no answer. Better to keep herself too busy to think and drive it from her mind. For six years she'd done a pretty good job of it, too—until today.

There was the sound of a truck coming down the road. Sadie cocked her head to listen. No one would be driving down that dirt road tonight unless he intended to come to the McClure farm.

The vehicle turned in at the gate, its headlights beaming a bright swath down the driveway. *That's why I was so restless,* Sadie admitted to herself. *I couldn't stop wondering if Reese would come back for that peach cobbler as Wynona had said he might.* She automatically reached to tidy her hair, then wished she'd changed clothes. She was still wearing the same white shorts and bare-midriff top.

The truck motor stopped, the lights went off, the door slammed. Sadie felt her pulse begin to flutter. This afternoon she'd noticed subtle changes in Reese. What changes had he found in her? She was grateful for the darkness that hid her from sight. Maybe tonight she would be safe from the intense scrutiny of his gaze.

Reese whistled as he walked at his usual fast pace from the pickup to the house. He was ready to bound up the steps when Sadie spoke.

"Nice evening, isn't it?" she said in a soft, almost shy voice.

She realized she'd surprised him.

In the darkness Reese sank down onto the wooden step beside her. "I just finished for the day and thought I'd check your mother on my way home. We had a transmission go out on one of the grain trucks." He leaned his head against the post and massaged his aching shoulders and neck. "It never fails at harvest time," he said wryly. "I always get to prove my mechanical skills out in a wheat field by the light of a lantern."

Sadie remembered that it took every vehicle working at the maximum to bring in the harvest. "Did you get it fixed?"

"Sure did. Took every cussword I've ever heard or read, but the truck's running again."

Sadie chuckled. Reese was like her father, using profanity the way women were reputed to use hairpins and chewing gum to perform magical repairs.

Reese reached for her hand and squeezed it. "It's good to hear the sound of your laughter again," he said. "I'd forgotten how much I missed it."

His hand was warm and callused around hers, and Sadie felt the strength of muscle and bone in his grip. In the old days he'd been able to hold fast to a bucking horse or lift a hundred-pound bag of seed with no effort. And yet how many times had he gently worked goathead stickers from Sadie's bare feet with those same hands? She turned her hand, palm up, inside his and felt the pulse that thrummed between them.

The night enveloped them in its dark, silent intimacy. Reese lifted his arm and wrapped it around her shoulders, then nudged her head in against his breastbone. The steady rhythm of his heartbeat pounded under her ear.

Sadie's tense muscles began to loosen. She felt safe and secure for the first time in a long time. She was home again, in the place where she belonged. She lifted her face.

"I've missed you, Reese," she said. "I didn't know how much until now."

Their lips met. It was a sweet, tender kiss, the kind shared by a couple of teenagers, bashful and hesitant, who kiss for the first time—a brief touching of lips. When she and Reese parted, Sadie's lashes were dusted with tears.

The night seemed to tremble in anxious anticipation. Something had happened during that kiss, but what? It's only my imagination, Sadie thought, even as some of her years-long struggle let go and was replaced by a sense of peace.

"Welcome home, Sadie." Reese's husky baritone was strained. "Tascosa is never the same without you."

Sadie experienced an unfamiliar timidity with Reese. She couldn't see his face and had no idea how he'd reacted to this kiss, which to her had seemed very special. There was something strange in his voice, but she couldn't identify it. Could it be the same anger he'd exhibited after he'd kissed her earlier that afternoon? The old confusion she always felt with Reese resurged, assaulting her mind.

"Let's go inside," Sadie said. "Wynona told me to save you some of her peach cobbler. I'll warm it up and put some ice cream on it for you."

Reese remained sitting on the steps. "My boots are full of chaff," he protested. "I don't want to track up the house. I'd better stay and eat it here, on the porch."

"It's not very comfortable on these steps." Sadie opened the screen door. "Remember how I always fussed at Daddy for not building a big porch on the house so we could have a porch swing, instead of having to sit on the steps?" The screen door slammed behind her.

Sadie returned a short while later and handed Reese a dish of peach cobbler. Its fruity, cinnamon odor mingled with the scent of honeysuckle that lay heavily on the night air. She sat down on the steps and took a bite of cobbler. "I still say someday I'm going to have a house with a real porch and a real swing—" She broke off to laugh at herself. "Funny, isn't it, how you never get over wanting some of the things you wanted when you were a kid? I'm twenty-eight years old and still wishing for an old-fashioned front porch."

Reese didn't respond to her comment. "Good cobbler," he said, spooning another bite into his mouth.

"Tom Evans is a lucky man. Wynona makes the best cobbler in the county."

"It always surprised me that Wynona married Tom," Sadie replied, a prickle of uncertainty making her uncomfortable with the new topic of conversation. She supposed she ought to leave well enough alone, but there were things she'd wondered about for a long time.

"Why is that?" Reese's voice seemed as cautious and tentative as Sadie's. "They'd known each other forever."

"Sure, but when we used to talk about the future, we figured I'd marry Jerry Don and she'd marry you."

Reese finished his cobbler before he spoke again. He seemed to be searching for words, the same way Sadie had done. "If you remember, we were more of a threesome than a foursome. Wynona didn't go to college with you and Jerry Don and me. While we were off at Texas Tech, she and Tom got pretty close."

Sadie's brow furrowed. "Reese, Wynona was my best friend. While the three of us were in college, Wynona and I wrote each other every week. I saw her every time I came home to visit on the weekends. I knew she and Tom were friends and went out together sometimes, but she *never* said anything to me about being in love with him."

"Maybe that was because he was older than the rest of us. She probably didn't want anyone to criticize him." Reese's spoon tapped against the rim of his empty dish.

"That doesn't explain why she'd keep a secret from her best friend." Sadie continued to probe the puzzle. "It's still a mystery to me when she fell in love with him."

"Well, if you see them together now, you won't have any doubt that she loves him. They're one of the happiest couples I've ever seen."

"Oh, I'm sure of that. I could tell by the way she talked this afternoon."

"Well, then," Reese replied as though that were the end of the matter. He reached behind them and shoved his empty dish across the porch, out of the way.

Sadie continued to puzzle over the matter. "But still, I just knew she'd marry you, Reese."

There was another silence. Then Reese uttered a bark of self-conscious laughter. "I gave her the chance."

"Yes, I know."

"She told you?" The words were surprised from Reese before he had a chance to censor them.

Sadie nodded her head, forgetting that Reese couldn't see the movement in the darkness. "The day after Jerry Don's funeral. She said you'd asked her, but later she wrote and told me she'd decided to marry Tom Evans instead." Sadie hesitated, then added, "I always figured that was why you rushed into marrying that girl in Chicago when you went up there to work as a cattle buyer. Rebound."

Reese stretched out his long legs. "Maybe you're right. I never thought about it that way before." He laughed wryly, in his typical way of steering a conversation away from all mention of personal feelings. "I thought it was because she was cute and sexy and winter was coming on in the Midwest. I wanted someone to snuggle with on a snowy night."

Sadie's lips curved into a smile. One of Reese's dearest traits was his ability to poke fun at himself. "Is that why your marriage broke up when summer came?" she asked, curious to know his response. She'd always wondered about that early, ill-fated marriage and why it had ended so soon. And why Reese had retreated and lived in solitary bachelorhood ever since.

"I guess so. I was young and foolish then." Reese gave a heavy mock sigh. "I hadn't learned a man wants to snuggle on a hot summer night just as much as he does in the winter." He turned toward her. In the starlight the contours of his face and shoulders were visible, but his expression was hidden. There was a hushed pause. Then he groaned and reached for her. "Damn it, on a summer night exactly like this one."

He crushed her body against his and buried his face in her neck. "You smell just the same," he whispered. "Like sunshine and roses." He found the hollow of her throat and began to kiss her—slow, lazy kisses that made her skin tingle. With his mouth he made his way to her ear and began to nibble at the lobe until she thrilled with arousal and leaned deeper into his embrace. Pleasurable sensations bombarded her body as his lips worked their magic, moving from her ear to her cheeks, then to her eyelids and up into her silky hair.

Reese shifted so that he was sitting upright on the top step, his legs apart. Sadie found herself moving from her sitting position to kneel on the step below Reese so that he could draw her body into the space between his knees. She leaned forward and wound her arms around his neck.

"Aren't you going to kiss me?" he whispered. "It's a hot summer night, just right for snuggling."

"We *are* snuggling," Sadie murmured, letting her fingers ripple through the thick hair at the base of his neck, then move down to stroke the firm muscles of his back.

"Sadie, please," he said, twisting his head to search for her mouth. "Kiss me."

She smiled against the cotton fabric of his open collar. She was surprised at how intoxicating it was to hear the urgent plea in his voice.

She stroked the front of Reese's shirt, kneading the chest muscles underneath. He was solidly built, with muscles powerful from a lifetime on the ranch. They both knew that anytime he wanted to, he could hold her as still as a helpless bird and kiss her to his heart's content. Sadie knew that her denial of the demanded kiss was just as exciting to Reese as it was to her. He was enjoying the challenge of melting her resistance.

"Just one little kiss. You don't have to do anything more unless you want to," he insisted, trying to catch her face between his hands and hold it still so he could kiss her.

She evaded him, laughing even as her heart began to race. "Are you making up the rules as you go along?" she asked. "How do I know you won't change them tomorrow?"

He nipped at her ear. "With you, Sadie, the ground is always shifting, and so are the rules. Let's don't worry about tomorrow until it gets here."

She gave a throaty laugh and let her body mold itself to his, her physical action contradicting the words that followed. "No kiss for you tonight, Mr. Chandler. Tomorrow, perhaps."

Reese moved his hands slowly, deliberately, down her back and bare waist, then cupped them around her bottom and pulled her forward until there was no distance at all separating them, nothing but thin layers of clothing.

The fierce contact made Sadie's breathing quicken. Murmuring incoherent sounds, Reese trailed his lips along her collarbone, then across the gentle swell at the open vee of her blouse. Sadie sucked in her breath. Desire ignited within her, and its consuming fires made her desperate for Reese's more intimate touch. With his finger he teasingly retraced the path made by his lips until it reached the center of her open neckline. Sadie felt overwhelmed by some unspoken need, and she waited tensely while his finger hesitated, suspended a fraction away from the pulsing tip of her breast. There was the slightest motion, so feathery she couldn't be sure whether he'd touched her or not. Then his lips brushed the crown of her head, and he uttered the self-satisfied laugh of a male who knows he's won an important victory.

"The next time we meet, Sadie, it's *you* who will be asking *me* for a kiss."

Before she could respond to his taunt, he was gone.

Chapter Three

Sadie didn't see Reese again for several days, and with the delay, confusion grew in her mind. She accepted at face value the reason Reese gave for his absence—that wheat had ripened in several fields simultaneously, and he'd be working almost around the clock trying to stay ahead of the weather. That necessity was typical during wheat-harvest season, because a sudden summer rainstorm could mean heavy losses. Still, Sadie thought it was just as well that Reese was tied up right now. He'd rekindled feelings in her that she'd thought were safely buried along with the past, and she wasn't sure how to deal with them. She was grateful for the interruption so that she could get her own thoughts in order.

Or so she told herself as she grew increasingly rest-less. The days seemed an eternity, though she stayed busy caring for her mother and trying to find ways to entertain her. Sadie played gin rummy and canasta, her mother's games of choice, until the cards were a blur. She and her mother caught up on all the television soap operas and all the local gossip. The physical inactivity began to wear on Sadie, and she found herself wishing she could ride horseback or take a swim or go waterskiing. Instead, she was trapped by her mother's need for care and company, so even with the temperature hovering above a hundred degrees, Sadie pitched into a frenzy of cleaning an already-spotless house. Late in the week she greeted Wynona from the top of a ladder, sweat trickling down her face as she washed the windows.

"Your mother's doing a lot better, Sadie, and she says you need a change of activities. I'll get Tom's teenage cousin to come take care of her on Saturday so you can come to our ten-year class reunion." Before Sadie could protest, Wynona insisted, "It'll be good for you to see everybody again, don't you think? You were always everybody's favorite, and you're still the prettiest. The reunion should be a real boost to your ego." There was a rueful chuckle as Wynona added, "Do you think I can lose twenty pounds by Saturday, hon?"

Sadie paused on the sidewalk in front of the high-school building to read a sign painted in large purple letters on a white banner draped across the entrance: Welcome, Tascosa High School Ten-year Class Reunion. A sudden gust of wind caught a tumbleweed and sent it rolling across the road in front of her. She'd been a lot like that tumbleweed, tossed in every direction by the shifting wind, Sadie thought. For a moment she considered turning around and going back home. It had been hard enough to see Reese and Wynona, her closest friends. Now she was going to have to go inside the high school and assume the sunshine personality everybody expected, be surrounded by all those painful memories of Jerry Don. Could she do it?

Another gust of wind blew past, and Sadie instinctively averted her head to minimize its effect on her long hair. She needed to look her best when she saw her former classmates. She was trying to smooth her loose curls back into place when the door of the school burst open and two energetic children darted past Sadie, almost knocking her off her feet.

"Aaron, I told you not to—" called an indignant voice from just inside the entry. "Why, look who's here! It's Sadie!" Her son's misadventures forgotten, Wynona hurried forward, followed by several classmates. Sadie was soon surrounded by old friends, all smiling and eager to wrap her in bear hugs.

"How wonderful to see you, Rose Alice! Is this your little boy with Aaron?"

"No, this rascal is Jimmy," Rose Alice answered. "He belongs to Wade and Sally. Would you believe they have five boys now! And I have my hands full with just one baby girl. Let me look at you," Rose Alice said when the boys had made a hasty retreat. "My goodness, you're more beautiful than ever. Life in the city must agree with you."

Sadie nodded. "I like Austin. There's always so much happening, and I stay busy. It makes the time go faster." Sadie toyed with the bright wooden ornaments that dangled from the belt of her green cotton-gauze top. When she realized that everybody was studying her face to look for changes, Sadie formed her lips into the dazzling smile that was her trademark. "What about you, Darlene?" she asked, turning to a quiet blonde in the group. "You're looking great—I can't wait to meet your husband." Darlene had been one of the few Tascosa graduates to marry an outsider, an oil-field worker from Midland.

Wynona looped an arm around Sadie's waist and led the group inside the building, then through the corridor to the clamor of voices in the gymnasium, where the homecoming committee had set up shop. Despite her inner anguish, which she carefully hid behind a perpetual smile, Sadie's interest in her classmates was genuine. She truly wanted to know about their spouses and children, the homes they'd established; and they were eager to tell her.

There had been forty-seven members of her graduating class. Except for the two who'd met early, tragic deaths, all the others had managed to return to Tascosa to celebrate their ten-year anniversary. Most of them had married young, and to each other. At least half of the married couples present had been high-school sweethearts and still lived in Tascosa, carrying on their family farms and businesses. A few had suffered disappointments and heartbreaks, and there had been a few divorces. But it seemed to Sadie, as she hugged first one and then another, that everyone except her had gotten married and started a family. She began to feel a nagging discomfort about the fact that she was still single.

"Sadie, look!" cried Darlene, urging her to read something she'd scribbled years before in an old yearbook. "Here you are, in your cheerleader outfit, waving your pom-pom."

"Here's Wynona, too. Look at those legs!" The book passed from hand to hand around the circle while Sadie and Wynona strutted in imitation of their photographic pose.

Someone turned the page. "There's the football team."

Everybody snickered. "Can you believe what Jerry Don did? I still don't know how he got away with it or how he got this picture past the yearbook sponsor."

The picture had been a cause célèbre at the time the book had been distributed, the week before graduation. Page fifty-nine of the Tascosa *Bulldogger* was notorious because Jerry Don Wallace, captain of the football team, had folded his arms across his chest like everyone else but then, at the instant the photograph was snapped, had formed an obscene gesture with his fingers. The hapless yearbook sponsor had nearly lost her job over the resulting fracas, and Jerry Don and his parents had spent some nervous hours in the principal's office when Jerry Don was threatened with a suspension that would have kept him from graduating,

"Mr. Peterson was so mad his face turned purple," someone remembered. "We thought he'd have a stroke."

"He's a good guy, though. He finally came around and let Jerry Don graduate. The school won't be the same without Mr. Peterson. He's retiring next month, Sadie. Had you heard?"

"Wynona mentioned it. She said he was going to make his retirement speech today." Sadie was glad to change the subject. It hurt too much to remember Jerry Don. When the group began to talk about other events, Sadie slipped away and began to play with one of the children.

Wynona noticed and went to join her friend. She squatted beside Sadie and put a sympathetic arm across her shoulders. "It's okay, Sadie."

"I knew his name would come up, but I didn't expect it to happen so soon. I've barely gotten here."

"Everybody loved Jerry Don," Wynona said softly, and Sadie could sense that tears were close to the surface for Wynona, too. "How can we have a reunion without remembering him? He's the one who made everything so much fun for the rest of us." She reached for Sadie's hand and squeezed it, then averted her face to hide the tears that trickled down her cheeks.

"I know." Sadie buried her face against the chubby two-year-old who was playing pat-a-cake with her. "Whose little girl is this? She's precious."

"Are you trying to change the subject?"

Sadie lifted stricken eyes to her friend. "Yes," she whispered.

"Does it always hurt you so much?"

"Not usually. I don't let myself think about him. But today is—"

"Yeah. Memories of Jerry Don are everywhere. It's hard to escape them." Wynona reached for a tissue and wiped her nose, then gave Sadie a shaky smile. "There's too much commotion in this gym to be able to think straight. The guys have got a barbecue pit going out by the softball field. Come on—let's go outside and see if we can find some lemonade or something."

Outside, the air was full of the delicious odor of Texas prime beef roasting over an open pit of banked coals. As Sadie and Wynona walked the fifty yards to the softball field, they could see a group of men giving their more-or-less undivided attention to huge sides of beef which were crusty now after hours of slow rotation on a spit, but still sizzling and popping onto the mesquite coals below. The air echoed with hearty male laughter as the men sipped keg beer in plastic cups and exchanged ribald jokes.

Someone caught sight of the two women headed their way and muttered, "Clean it up, fellows. Here come females."

The other men looked up with interest. "Well, I'll be damned...."

"So she did come after all...."

A wolf whistle pierced the air. "Sadie!"

"Wade, I can't breathe," Sadie protested, laughing as she tried to extricate herself from a fierce hug.

Wade reluctantly loosened his hold, then surrendered her to the man on his right.

"Charlie, how wonderful to see you!" Sadie exclaimed to the next man who hugged her. "Look how tanned you are. Have you been working in the fields?"

"Wheat harvest. Bumper crop this year. We've been operating the combine by floodlight, working till midnight all week long so we could take today off."

Sadie greeted each one in turn, looking for the boy she'd known in each face. They had the features of men now, with jaws that had lost their early roundness and become squared, with new lines at mouth and eyes to betray the hard times they'd all known sometime or other in these past ten years. They've changed, she thought. But she had changed, too. That was not the kind of thought she could permit herself, though; not today, not when it was taking all her strength to get through this class reunion and its reminders of Jerry Don.

She turned to Wade with a smile. "I'm famished, Wade. Do you think you could sneak me a bite of that barbecue?"

"Sure thing." He put his arm around her and led her to the spit. "Let me see if I can find a knife, and I'll slice you off a chunk." Wade turned, his body no longer blocking her view of the spit. "Hey, Reese, where'd you put that knife?"

Reese Chandler tensed.

Sadie, too, stood still. So Reese was already here. She'd known she'd run into him sometime today and have to deal with the feelings he'd aroused in her the other evening. But not now, not so soon, not when she was still reeling from the memories of Jerry Don. Yet she dared not let the moment lengthen. People were watching. What would be the normal way for Jerry Don's girl and Jerry Don's best friend to greet each other? Sadie shuddered inside. This was going to be the hardest moment of all. After this, the rest would be a piece of cake.

She looked up. Reese was walking toward her, the sun at his back so that the brim of his cowboy hat cast a shadow over the top half of his face. He towered above her, his body as long-legged and lean as ever, his walk the same lithe, easy amble. He was no more than three steps from her now, and still she couldn't see his eyes. She felt exposed, vulnerable, for the same sun from which Reese was protected beat full upon her own face, its brightness spotlighting the emotions she wanted to conceal.

She hurried forward. She didn't know where it came from, but somehow she managed to produce a smile and lightly flung herself against Reese's chest even as he extended his right hand to shake hers. "Reese," she murmured. "How nice to see you."

"Glad you changed your mind and decided to come to the reunion," he said in a matter-of-fact voice. "How's your mom doing today?" Reese clenched her fingers too tightly, and Sadie made a soft sound of protest. "Sorry," he muttered, letting go of her hand. He bent and brushed a kiss against the top of her head, a kiss so light that Sadie scarcely felt it.

What is he thinking about? Sadie wondered. Reese acted as though nothing had happened between them the other night. She'd have to be careful to act the same way.

"Will you give Sadie a bite of that barbecue?" asked Wade. "She says she's starving." He bumbled around, creating enough confusion to break the tension, and made a big production of slicing off a sizzling piece of beef. Wade waved the portion on a fork, waiting for it to cool, then offered it to Sadie.

The crowd broke up, as everybody was ready now for a game of softball, and several men went back to the school building to hunt up the equipment in the gym.

"What's this about hitting two home runs?" Reese said, joining the conversation.

"That's my goal." Sadie could ride horseback, swim, water-ski, snow ski, run a mile in under ten minutes, and had even been known to sky dive and go up in a hot-air balloon. Surely she could hit two home runs.

"How long has it been since you've played softball?"

"Oh, a while."

"Then what makes you think you can hit two home runs? You're not in the minors, now, McClure—this is big league, you hear me?" The men were taking pleasure in taunting Sadie.

"I told you. I've been practicing my swing."

"You know who our pitcher is?" Wade pointed at Reese Chandler. "Right there. You think you're going to get two home runs off of ol' Reese? Not on your sweet life, you ain't."

Reese slouched on one leg and stared at Sadie. For the first time, she could see his eyes. A shiver ran up her spine. It was the same expression that had troubled her thoughts these past few days.

Sadie turned away. "I'm off to find a bat. I intend to hit those home runs. It's a point of honor."

"We'll see, McClure, we'll see." Reese raised his right arm and began rotating it, practicing the motions for his pitch. "I'm going to go loosen up."

Point of honor or no, Sadie didn't hit two home runs. She hit one triple with bases loaded, one single, one pop fly to center field, and one home run with no one on base. By the time they'd played nine grueling innings, her hair was wind tossed and damp with perspiration, her perky green outfit grimy from sliding onto the dirt mound at third base. She had skinned her arm and scraped one knee and knew she'd be so sore she'd never be able to get out of bed the next day. She limped over to home plate to shake Reese's hand. "Great pitching," she said, wiping sweat from her forehead.

"Nice batting," he answered, never one to overstate things or embellish them.

"What do you mean, 'nice'? I'd say batting seven fifty isn't too bad for an ol' gal who's out of shape."

"You've never been out of shape in your life."

"My aching muscles tell me otherwise. I'm going to go and get some clean clothes from the trunk of my car. Do you think the water's turned on in the girls' gym so I can take a shower?"

"The water's probably on, but if you take a shower, you do it at your own risk. Don't you remember all the stories about how guys would line up at the side of the building and peek in the windows?"

"They always bragged about doing it, but I never believed them."

"Believe it. It's true." At fifteen, Reese himself had been one of the ones who peeked. Not that the boys could see anything through the smoked glass, but it had certainly provided titillating conversation for days afterward.

"Reese," Sadie protested, "what am I going to do? I'm a mess. I can't go around smelling like a wet dog for the rest of the day. I've *got* to take a shower and get cleaned up."

"Let me know when you get back with your clothes and I'll keep a lookout for you while you shower."

"How do I know you won't peek yourself?"

His grin was devilish. "You don't."

Chapter Four

If Reese Chandler peeked when Sadie was in the girls' shower, he never let on. Somehow Sadie thought she could rely on his gentlemanly instincts. She took her time scrubbing down and soaping her hair, and finally emerged from the gym in a T-shirt and cutoffs, her hair damp and pulled back.

"Feeling better?" asked Reese. She looked so fresh and innocent that he wanted to reach out to touch the dewy skin, the damp reddish-gold ringlets. Instead, he tilted his hat to shade his eyes. "You ready to go get something to eat? They rang the dinner bell while you were in the shower."

"We'd better hurry to get in line, then. I want to be sure to try every fabulous-looking dish." Sadie patted her stomach as they made their way to rejoin the others. "I'll have to run ten miles before I go to bed tonight, but it'll be worth it."

The men had carried the long cafeteria tables out into the breezeway, and the women had been piling large bowls of food on them all morning. The barbecued meat had been sliced and arranged on platters, and in addition there were grilled hot dogs and hamburgers, the preferred children's food items. There were frosty pitchers of iced tea and lemonade, ice chests full of canned soft drinks, and another keg of beer. In short, it was a feast, with so much food that it was impossible to sample everything.

Everyone had spread blankets under the mulberry and cottonwood trees and settled down to serious eating by the time Sadie and Reese arrived. Wynona called Sadie's name and pointed them in the direction of a spare blanket spread by itself in the semiprivacy of a honeysuckle vine. Sadie hesitated before sitting down away from the others, but everywhere she looked, she saw families and couples with no room to spare. Once again she had the same strange feeling that had pricked her earlier in the morning. Unmarried, she felt like a fifth wheel in the midst of all this connubial fellowship. She wondered if Reese felt the same way. It must be worse for him, really. At least in Austin, Sadie had single friends. Here in Tascosa, Reese was the only unmarried person under the age of fifty.

With her muscles already beginning to ache, she sank onto the blanket. Reese lowered himself beside her and handed her an extra dish of peach cobbler, then stretched out his long body to face hers. The fragrance of the honeysuckle was intoxicating. She stretched out on her side, propped her head on one elbow, and enjoyed the breeze against her skin while she savored her first bite of the delicious meal.

"What are you thinking about?" Reese asked. "You have a faraway look in your eyes."

"Nothing. Everything." Sadie smiled. In the depths of Reese's eyes, Sadie saw something more than the ancient sadness he'd tried to hide from her, but she didn't recognize what it was. She felt a strange stirring of her heart. There was something vulnerable about Reese that she'd never noticed before. But had she ever really looked at him? He'd always been so quiet, so easygoing, always in Jerry Don's shadow; but Reese had never been anything more to her than, well, than Reese: steady and dependable, soft-spoken, a loyal friend.

No, that wasn't strictly true. Once, just once, he'd been something more than a friend. But she couldn't think about that today. She shook her head to drive away the memory. *Close your eyes now, quickly, before he sees the tears.*

"Sadie..."

In another moment he'd reach out and touch her, and then she'd be undone. If she started crying, she'd never be able to stop. She deliberately took a sip of iced tea and forced her throat to swallow. She performed her old trick for times of panic; inside her head she recited the names of the presidents in order, beginning with George Washington. By the time she got to Theodore Roosevelt, she'd regained control.

She shuddered. Why had she let her mother and Wynona talk her into coming to this class reunion, anyway? She should have known she wasn't ready to deal with all these old memories. Maybe she would never be ready. She'd made a dreadful mistake. How was she going to get herself out of here before she fell apart? If people would only begin to stir, she could make an excuse about her mother and go home. But nobody was inclined to move after the rigors of the softball game and a full meal. From the other side of the honeysuckle vine, Sadie could hear the sound of snoring. Would this day never end?

"You haven't tasted your cobbler," Reese said.

"I'm afraid I don't have room for it." Sadie looked at the bowl of dessert. She'd choke if she tried to take a single bite of it. "Would you like to have it?" She handed it to Reese.

"Well, only if you insist."

Her fingers were icy as they touched his, she knew.

"You look tired, Sadie. Wouldn't you like to take a nap for a while?"

"Oh, yes, I would. You won't think I'm rude?" If only she could lie here with her eyes closed, without the need to make conversation or try to appear normal, then maybe she could endure the remainder of the day.

"Nope. Turn around here, so you'll be in my shadow. You don't want your nose to sunburn." Following his instructions, Sadie shifted her body to curve against his. "Here, put your head on my shoulder. The ground's so hard you'll get a crick in your neck."

Sadie was too far gone to protest. All she wanted was peace and privacy, an almost impossible desire in the midst of this crowd. She laid her head on Reese's outstretched arm and worked herself into a comfortable position, nestled against the hollow of his shoulder. His body was hard and strong against her back. She closed her eyes, then felt him cock the brim of his hat so it shaded her face. His free hand moved to her neck and began to knead it gently. She thought he murmured something, but she didn't catch the words. Sooner than she expected, she escaped into a peaceful sleep.

An hour later she awakened to the sound of children shouting. More resilient than their parents, they'd rested long enough and were ready for physical activity.

Sadie yawned, stretched, and felt a temporary sense of dislocation. Gradually she became aware of her surroundings, felt the warmth of the body touching hers, the strong forearm that supported her head. She turned onto her back and looked up into Reese's face, which was shaded as usual by the brim of his hat.

"How long did I sleep? Your arm must be numb."

The numbness had given way to needle pricks of pain a half hour earlier, but Reese didn't admit that to Sadie. Instead, he smiled down at her, and if there was an unusual expression in his eyes, he knew Sadie couldn't be sure because of the shadows that hid his face from view.

She lifted herself and shook her hair into place. "Did you take a nap, too?"

"I guess I might have dozed a little."

"What's on the agenda for the rest of the afternoon?" Sadie could hear people stirring now, and knew the quiet part of the day was over. She needed to get her emotional defenses back in place.

"Horseshoes, I think, and volleyball. I think someone set up a croquet court. When it gets dark, there's going to be a fireworks show for the kids." Reese raised himself and sat cross-legged, facing her. "Would you like something cold to drink? That sun is really getting hot."

"Help me up, and I'll go with you. Some iced tea would taste pretty good."

Reese stood, offered Sadie his callused hand, and tugged till she was on her feet.

Her muscles protested with every move, and her scraped knee almost refused to bend. "I think I'm going to have to find an activity that doesn't require any exertion. I'm not even sure I can walk."

"Sure you can. Lean on me. We've got to work the soreness out of that knee so you can run the three-legged race."

Reese grinned at her as they both recalled Seniors Day, when the two of them had won the three-legged race.

"I think that must've been your happiest day in high school, the day we beat Jerry Don and took home the trophy," Sadie commented.

"Well, I didn't get too many chances to leave Jerry Don in the dust. Not that I didn't try. All the time." Reese's arm fell loosely across Sadie's shoulders to support her as she hobbled across the school yard.

"You two were a strange pair of friends. You'd do or die for each other, you'd fight each other's fights, but you never stopped competing with each other, either. I don't know what would've happened if they hadn't declared a tie and named both of you Most Valuable Player."

She was right, Reese knew. They'd never stopped competing. Never. Not even now. Jerry Don had been dead for six years, and Reese was still competing with his ghost. Reese's jaw clenched, but he said nothing. He didn't want to talk to Sadie about that strange rivalry he'd had with his best friend, the guy he'd truly loved like a brother. Reese glanced at the picnic table. It was surrounded with people, everybody thirsty at the same time. Good. There'd be plenty of other people to carry on the conversation. He'd said enough for one day.

Dusk fell late in the Panhandle. It was almost nine o'clock when the sun had worked its way to the western horizon of the prairie and set the sky ablaze. Sadie hadn't seen such a sunset in a long time, and she'd forgotten how it simply took one's breath away. She lay back on the blanket, arms folded beneath her head, and gazed heavenward, saying nothing.

Reese lay beside her, chewing on a stalk of wheat. Wynona's eldest son, Aaron, sat with them, excited that darkness was finally coming so they could have their fireworks.

"It's dark, Mommy. Please, let's start the fireworks," Aaron cried to Wynona, who sat on a nearby blanket.

"Not yet, son. We have to wait till the stars come out."

"Mommy, no, please, we'll have to wait *forever*. Can't we light the sparklers? Please, let us start."

Other children took up the hue and cry, so the parents opened up packages of ladyfingers—long strings of tiny firecrackers on a single fuse that popped merrily for a long time. They went over to the sidewalk, careful to light the firecrackers on the pavement so there wouldn't be any stray sparks to start a grass fire.

Darkness began to set in, and the older children were allowed to set off Roman candles and pop-bottle rockets. The adults sat on the blankets and watched, slapping at the occasional mosquito. When the heavens became totally black except for the myriads of twinkling stars, the parents brought out the serious fireworks, the ones that exploded high in the sky with shooting stars and bright colors. At each display, the crowd would applaud and cheer. The children sat, openmouthed and awed, completely bedazzled by the wonder of it all.

Someone brought a stereo from the gym and a stack of favorite records saved from their high-school days. Music began to play, and as the fireworks ended and the children drifted off to sleep on the blankets, the adults began to dance.

Sadie and Reese had been watching from the sidelines, both of them now wary of the intimacy of dancing together. As they watched, however, married couples moved closer together, bodies clinging as memories were stirred. There was a growing sensuality that was almost palpable, and Sadie and Reese began to feel isolated.

"Come on," Reese said gruffly, taking Sadie's hand. "Let's dance. It's about time for a fast number. Let's show them what real dancing is."

Someone changed the record to a fast-moving country-and-western number that had been one of their high-school favorites. A great athlete because of his superb sense of timing, Reese was also quite a dancer. Sadie was his equal, and before they knew it, everybody else had dropped to the sidelines to watch. They did six dances nonstop, then fell against each other, breathless.

The pace changed with another album of slow songs, and soon everybody else was dancing again. Sadie's head nestled against Reese's shoulder as their bodies moved in unison to the rhythm. His arms loosely cradled her as they hummed the words. She'd forgotten his wonderful baritone voice. "This is nice," she murmured.

His hand tightened slightly around her waist, but he said nothing.

"In the dark, you can almost pretend that nothing has changed and that we're all eighteen again," Sadie said.

"Would you want to go back?" His feet circled in a fast step that surprised her, but she kept up with the rhythm.

"There are some things I'd do differently. I've made some mistakes."

"We all have. That's the way life is."

"But whatever mistakes you've made haven't changed you, Reese. You're still the same."

Reese swung her wide, then drew her back against his chest on the next beat of the song. "What about you, Sadie? Are you so different from the girl you used to be?"

"What do you think?" She was curious. To herself she seemed so much older, more cynical. She did a quick half step and almost lost the beat until Reese steadied her.

"You seem more restless. You're too thin, and I don't remember that you used to be so moody."

She gave a wry chuckle. "That's because you've always been moody enough for both of us. You expected me to be Little Miss Sunshine even when you were a black thundercloud."

"Is that all that's different?"

"I suppose I'm more nervous today," she admitted. "It's a strain to come back and try to pick up the pieces when I haven't seen everybody in so long."

The song ended, and they glided to a stop in the shadow of the building. Instead of rejoining the others, they lingered in the darkness.

"You seem tired." Reese reached out and gently touched the lines at the corners of her eyes, the concern in his voice inviting her to be honest with him.

Her hair swirled as she nodded. "It's coming back here and realizing how different everything is, how different *I* am. It scares me. I don't know what's happening to me." Her fingers tightened their grip on his hand, which still rested beside her lips. "I'm having a hard time today. Everybody else in our class has settled down and built a life. All I have is a bunch of dead hopes and faded dreams." She buried her face against his chest, aghast at the stream of words, raw in their honesty, that had bubbled forth, unbidden.

Reese held her close, trying to comfort her with the warmth and strength of his body. For a moment he thought she might be weeping, but then he realized that she was beyond tears, lost in some strange terror that he couldn't understand. He rocked her in his arms, murmuring against her ear until he felt her tension lessen.

She pulled away and looked up into his face, her eyes stricken with some dreadful emotion. "Why can't I let go of Jerry Don so I can fall in love with someone else?'' she whispered, demanding comfort for her inner grief. ''I want to get married and have a family, too, but I can't—not until I'm free of Jerry Don's ghost.''

Reese turned his head, gazing across the moonlit prairie at wheat fields silhouetted against the horizon. He wanted so much to say the right thing. In his desperation to console her, he choked on the only words he could find. ''Sadie, any man would be lucky to have you for his wife, even if Jerry Don always keeps his place in your heart.'' He turned to her and with slow deliberation gripped her shoulders, pulling her body tightly against his. Then he moved his hands upward, cupping her cheeks and tilting her face to his. ''You're the most beautiful woman in the world, Sadie McClure, and you always will be.''

He lowered his mouth to hers even as he tightened his arms and lifted her against the strength of his body. His lips plundered hers, trying to satisfy in this single moment the yearnings of a lifetime. His breathing was ragged now, and he was lost in time and space as he crushed her lips until she parted them, allowing his tongue into her dark, sweet recesses. He groaned as he cradled her hips and pulled her against him. His hands moved from her hips to the warm, soft mounds of her bosom.

Sadie sighed at the feelings Reese stirred in her, and tightened her arms around his neck. He reached under her T-shirt and stroked with an insistent rhythm until she felt the heat raging in her body. If they'd had another second of privacy, they would have made love right there, creating their own private version of Fourth of July fireworks. But that was not to be, because the music had ended and their married friends, who had experienced a similar kind of arousal, were eager to go home.

Couples began to drift to their cars, with sleepy children slung over their father's shoulders, and there were the soft calls of "Good night, see you later," to mark the end of the evening. No one could see Sadie and Reese, sheltered as they were in the shadow of the building, but the two heard the departures and began a slow trip back to sanity.

Sadie straightened her clothes, still overwhelmed by the sensations Reese had stirred in her.

"I apologize, Sadie," he muttered.

"It's okay, Reese. Don't worry about it. I—" She broke off. She'd been about to say, *I wanted you, too. I wanted the comfort of another human being to push back the darkness.* But this wasn't the time for words like that.

"Yeah." He turned to go.

"Reese?"

"Yes?" He stood, waiting.

Sadie said nothing. But she stood on tiptoe and lightly brushed his lips with hers.

Chapter Five

Just before dawn, the soft trill of a mockingbird nudged Sadie awake. She rolled onto her stomach and buried her head in the pillows, but it was too late. Sleep had vanished, chased away by a rising sense of unease. The class reunion yesterday had taken its toll as a roller-coaster emotional ride, and now Sadie had to deal with the aftereffects. With a sigh she sat up in bed, wadding the pillows to support her back, then brushed her fingertips across her bruised, tingling lips.

What had happened to make Reese kiss her with such savage tenderness? And what had caused her to make that desperate, almost wanton response? Some primitive, mutual need had seized them in its grasp, then hurtled them into a whirling abyss of sensation.

Her cheeks flamed with embarrassment at the memory. What had come over her? She remembered Reese's magic touch, the combined strength and gentleness in the hands that all too briefly explored her body, and experienced anew the pleasure he'd awakened in her. She stretched sensuously underneath the light covers, letting her toes wiggle, and realized she'd have to guard herself in any future meetings with Reese. The feelings he'd aroused in her were too powerful, too tempting, to resist. With that resolve in mind, she tossed back the covers and went to take a shower.

Later, when Sadie carried steaming cups of coffee into her mother's bedroom, Nelda seemed to be feeling much better. "You know, Sadie, I think it would be good for me to get out of the house for a while. I'm not used to being cooped up like this."

Sadie gave her mother a thoughtful look. "Your color is much better. Are you strong enough to walk down to the cottonwood trees? I could take our breakfast down there."

"What I'd really like to do is go to church, Sadie. Everybody's been too busy with the wheat harvest to drop by to visit, and I'm missing my friends. They'll all be at the church service." Nelda tossed back the sheet and reached for her crutches.

"Mom, are you sure? I'm afraid you're rushing things."

"I want to go, Sadie. This is Sunday, and I wouldn't feel right if I missed the service again. I promise, I'll be just fine." Nelda had the same determined tilt to her jaw that Sadie had inherited.

"I'm not sure I can get you into my car with that cast on your leg." Sadie was still looking for an excuse. She didn't want her mother to overextend herself. "I could never lift you into your pickup."

For a moment Nelda looked confused, then she brightened. "We can call Reese. He won't mind helping."

Sadie tried to still the sudden pounding of her pulse. "I'm sure he's going to be busy in the fields today, Mom. He said last night he was behind schedule."

Nelda reached for the bedside telephone and dialed a number. "It won't hurt anything to ask," she insisted. "Reese is just like my own son. He'll help if he can." Nelda leaned back in the rocking chair and studied Sadie with a disconcerting expression. "I'm glad you and Reese are having this chance to renew your friendship. I'd always hoped the two of you would—Reese, is that you? Listen, dear, would you mind doing me a favor?"

Sadie glanced around the small community church that formed the center of Tascosa's social and religious life. She hadn't attended a service in years, yet little had changed. The same people sat in the same pews, and the congregation sang the same hymns. The only noticeable difference was Wynona, rocking a sleepy baby in her arms while Tom tried to quiet their three toddlers. How many years had it been since Sadie and Wynona had sat in the back pew, whispering and passing notes to their school chums? Back then, who would ever have thought they'd end up this way, with Wynona a mother of four and Sadie a career woman, still single at twenty-eight? Sadie shifted uncomfortably in her seat and bumped against Reese's shoulder, close beside hers.

"Sorry," she murmured, shifting again and forcing her gaze to wander to the stained-glass windows, the organ, the hymnbooks—anything to get her mind off the distracting presence beside her. She leaned in the opposite direction, toward her mother. "Doing okay, Mom?"

Nelda smiled and nodded, then patted Sadie's hand. "Isn't it wonderful for us to be here together, like a family again?" Nelda whispered. "It's nice to have Reese sitting in your father's place."

Sadie swallowed hard and hoped Reese hadn't heard. Why did her mother get these crazy ideas into her head, anyway? It had become increasingly obvious during Sadie's visit that her mother was busy matchmaking. Apparently the fall and the broken leg had made Nelda do some stocktaking about growing old. She no longer seemed resigned to Sadie's absence from Tascosa and had begun waging a not-too-subtle campaign to bring her daughter back home.

Sadie expelled her breath in a soft sigh. On her right sat Reese, with his disturbing effect, and on her left sat her mother, with a dominating stubbornness. As folks from Tascosa would say, Sadie was caught between a rock and a hard place. She felt an enormous relief when the minister said the benediction. Before people began to gather around and exchange greetings, Sadie muttered an excuse and made her escape through the side door. She wasn't in the mood to listen to her mother tell everyone how wonderful it was to have Sadie home again.

Even on the hot July day, there was a slight breeze against Sadie's cheek. Her heart raced as though she'd run half a mile, and she looked for a place of solitude where she could compose herself from the feelings that threatened to overcome her. Down below the church was the community cemetery, sheltered in a grove of cottonwood trees with leaves shimmering silver in the rustling wind. By instinct she made her way to her father's grave and stood gazing down at his headstone:

James Barton McClure
Beloved Husband and Father
Good and Wise Friend to All Who Knew Him
Now at Home in Glory

Sadie squeezed her hands into a fist and dug her nails into her palms. She felt an aching loneliness she'd never known before. Surrounded by her parents' love, she hadn't minded being an only child, especially because she'd always had Jerry Don and Reese for playmates. Now Reese had more or less disappeared from her life, and Jerry Don was gone forever. Mom was too weak for Sadie to lean on anymore, and there was no one else who mattered. She hugged her arms around her slim body and walked to the other side of the cemetery, where Jerry Don was buried. Growing by his headstone was a mass of bright orange marigolds, as perky and impervious to the hot Texas sun as Jerry Don himself had been.

She knelt to pick one of the blossoms, then crushed its petals and sprinkled them over his grave. "I loved you, Jerry Don," she whispered to the spirit that haunted her. In memory she could see him, smiling broadly with dimples twinkling, young and tanned with his blond hair sun bleached nearly to silver. She could almost hear him call her name in the same old way, his voice rippling with laughter as he coaxed her to join him in one of his daredevil pranks. "I always loved you, Jerry Don," Sadie whispered. "I always will. Please believe me, won't you? All those arguments we had at the end were *because* I loved you so much and I didn't want anything to hurt you." Tears slid down her cheeks. "There was never anyone else for me but you. We would've gotten married and had a bunch of kids and lived happily ever after. So why did you have to wrap your Thunderbird around a tree and leave me alone like this? It isn't fair!" She buried her face in her hands and sobbed.

"Hey, don't cry, Sadie, please don't cry." Before she could react to his unexpected appearance and turn to face him, Reese was kneeling beside her. He wrapped her in his arms and pulled her into the shelter of his chest, lightly stroking her hair while she cried herself out. "There, there," he crooned, "don't be sad, sweetheart." His breath was soft against her ear, his hands gentle against the curve of her back. "Don't think about the bad times, Sadie. Remember the good times, the way Jerry Don would want you to remember him. Remember how much joy he gave us and forget the rest, Sadie. Forget it, or you'll break your heart."

"I can't forget, Reese. I can't." Her tears soaked the front of his shirt, and she searched the pocket of her sundress for a tissue.

"Here," he said, taking out his handkerchief and wiping her cheeks. "How many times have I done this for you?" he asked, giving her an abashed grin. "Every time you fell and scraped your knee, it was ol' Reese who bandaged it and wiped the tears from your face."

Surprise diverted Sadie's attention. "I never thought about it before. I guess you were the one who always looked after me."

"Somebody had to. Otherwise you'd have followed Jerry Don off every cliff he decided to leap from. By the time we were in the sixth grade, I knew if anybody was going to save that pretty neck of yours from getting broken, it would have to be me. Here. Blow."

Sadie blew, noisily. With anyone else she might have felt self-conscious, but not with Reese.

"Feeling better?" he asked.

She nodded, then glanced down at the grass-covered mound. "Even after all these years, it's hard to believe he's really dead. I've never known anyone else who was so totally alive."

Reese gave her shoulder a casual squeeze, then got to his feet. "That's our Jerry Don. Beside him, everyone else looked like a feeble imitation of life."

"Not you, Reese," Sadie protested as she offered her hand for him to pull her to her feet.

"You can't fool someone who knows you as well as I do, Sadie, so don't try. Jerry Don and I weren't even in the same league where you were concerned."

"That's not true, Reese. You know you were always my best friend. Besides, you and Jerry Don were a lot alike, always competing in sports, trying to outdo each other. I can never think of one of you anymore without thinking of the other."

"Maybe that's part of the problem, Sadie. You've buried both of us in the same grave. The only problem is that I'm still alive."

Sadie lifted her head to find Reese's eyes turned glacier cold. "I don't understand what you're talking about," she said, feeling a strange tightening in her throat.

"I don't suppose you do. You won't let yourself."

Sadie was positive there was anger in Reese's voice. "Won't you explain?"

"Your mother is waiting for us. We need to get her home to bed before she has a setback." Before Sadie could catch up with him, Reese had jumped the picket fence and left her to make her way from the cemetery alone.

An unusual quiet had fallen over the McClure house. Nelda, exhausted, was sleeping soundly. Reese had left long ago, presumably to work in the fields. He'd had little to say as he returned Sadie and her mother home from church. Sadie was alone now, and the silence was closing in. She boiled an egg and made herself a chef's salad with fresh spinach from the garden, then ate scarcely a half-dozen bites. It must be the heat, she decided. She flipped through the channels on the television set and found nothing interesting. She picked up the telephone to call Wynona, then realized her friend would be busy putting the children down for their naps. Sunday afternoon was no time to call a harried young mother of four.

She slipped outside, wishing once again for a shady front porch with a swing. The steps were in full sun, and it was too hot to linger there. She made her way to the far corner of the yard, into the grove of cottonwoods, and lay down in the soft grass. From somewhere she could hear the distant whirring of a cicada, but otherwise the world was silent. She rolled over and buried her face in the grass, enjoying its texture against her cheek. The scent reminded her of long-ago grass fights with Reese and Jerry Don, and all at once pain welled within her so powerfully that she was helpless to force it back.

She rolled her body into a tight ball and felt dry, racking sobs tear through her. Jerry Don. Reese. The argument. The wreck. The funeral. Wynona. Reese. Jerry Don. "No!" she cried aloud. "Jerry Don, don't torture me anymore. Please, I didn't mean to hurt you. Forgive me, and give me peace." In the silence, no one heard her cry. But the memories, once started, could not be checked, and her mind whirled dizzily until it arrived at the central core of her guilt: the last time she saw Jerry Don alive....

"Got any more beer in the refrigerator?" Jerry Don asked, sprawled half drunk on the couch in his college apartment. The stereo was blaring heavy-metal music, and competing with it was a rerun of a boxing match on TV.

"I think you drank it all," Sadie answered, holding one hand against her ear to block out some of the noise. "I'm trying to study for finals."

Jerry Don reached for her hand and pulled her onto the couch with him. "Come on, Sadie, we're going to get married in two months." He gave her a moist kiss that tasted like the beer he'd been drinking all afternoon.

Sadie brushed his lips with a light kiss and tried to smile. "You're such a sweet guy when you're sober, Jerry Don. Why do you have to spoil everything by drinking too much?"

"Look, I don't want to argue about my drinking today, okay?"

"It's because I love you, Jerry Don." She stroked his cheekbone with her thumb until his blue eyes lost their clouded anger and began to twinkle again. "There's nobody like you when you're being your real self."

And it was true. Sober, Jerry Don had all the endearing traits of a seven-year-old boy with charm enough to coax a fox from its lair. But even at his best, he needed Sadie's total attention and encouragement. He'd fallen behind the competition during their college years, and it was devastating to his ego to find himself in second place at anything. Sadie had discovered that nurturing Jerry Don through the disappointments of early adulthood would be a full-time job. Yet somehow the greater his need for her became, the more love she had for him.

"There's not a guy on campus who doesn't envy me for being engaged to you, Sadie. They all want you, but I'm the lucky guy who's got you. Ol' Reese may have wound up being captain of the football team, but he couldn't take you away from me. You're one thing he didn't win."

"That's crazy, Jerry Don. Reese is our best friend. *Our* best friend. He always will be."

"Yeah, well, he'd better keep his hands off you, that's all I can say." Jerry Don tried to coax Sadie into a long, intimate kiss, but she broke away. "Guess I don't have to worry about that, though. You'd be just as icy with Reese as you are with me, wouldn't you?"

Sadie pulled herself out of reach. "Two months isn't long. We can wait."

"Maybe *you* can. It's not that easy for *me*." He got up and went into the kitchen. "You lied to me, Sadie. There's another six-pack in here."

Sadie went into the kitchen to join Jerry Don. "Why don't we cook some supper? You don't need any more beer tonight, Jerry Don."

"Damn it, Sadie, will you quit telling me what I need? I'm a grown man, and I can figure out for myself what I need and what I don't need. Leave me alone, for God's sake!" He sat down at the kitchen table and flipped the top of another can of beer, then took a deep swallow.

Sadie slid onto an adjoining chair, utterly dejected. "Jerry Don, I just don't think I can handle your drinking anymore. I think maybe we ought to postpone our wedding for a while until things get better between us. We don't want to make a big mistake."

"You think it would be a mistake to marry me when we've been in love since we were twelve years old? What are you talking about, Sadie?"

"I love the person you used to be, Jerry Don. I'm not so sure about the person you turn into sometimes. It scares me into thinking that you're going to change permanently and we'll end up making each other miserable."

When he turned on all his charm, Jerry Don could be very convincing. He'd manipulated her before, but this time Sadie braced herself. She held firm, and they continued to talk for another half hour. Finally, though, she accepted defeat. "You won't even try to change?"

"Not now, baby, not with finals coming up and everything. When we get back from our honeymoon, then I'll stop drinking. Or cut way down. You'll see."

Sadie twisted her engagement ring from her finger and held it out to him. "I guess I'm not willing to take that chance, Jerry Don. I love you, but I can't marry you. Not now. You're going to have to quit drinking first, and then we'll see."

His face flushed crimson with anger, and he took the ring and threw it across the room. "Like hell," he shouted. "There's plenty of women who'd give their eyeteeth to be in your place, Sadie. I can get along just fine without you, and I don't need a wife who doesn't trust me." He got up from the table and stormed to the front door.

Sadie jumped up and followed him, tears streaming down her cheeks. "Jerry Don, don't," she cried, trying to stop him. "You've had too much to drink. Don't go. Please, let's talk."

But her words were fruitless. He pushed her aside and slammed the door behind him. Before she could follow him down the stairs, his car was roaring out of the parking lot, its tires squealing.

Chapter Six

Sadie sat up in the grass and wiped her eyes on her shirttail, thinking that she'd shed more tears on this trip home to Tascosa than in all the rest of her life put together. What had happened to her famous sunshiny disposition? For six years it had served as a barrier to hold back her pain, but now the walls had come tumbling down. Once started, the tears wouldn't stop.

Remembering the last time she'd seen Jerry Don alive, Sadie knew her conscience would hurt even if her actions hadn't ended with breaking their engagement. But instead, she'd magnified her guilt by what she'd done during the hour following his stormy exit, before news had come that Jerry Don was dead. If only Reese hadn't arrived just when he did. There must have been some terrible jinx hanging over that day to make every good intention turn sour. For of course it was perfectly normal for Reese to return to the apartment he shared with Jerry Don. What wasn't normal was for him to find Sadie on her hands and knees on the kitchen floor, crying her eyes out while she looked for the engagement ring that had been tossed aside. . . .

"What's wrong, Sadie?" Reese asked, squatting beside her on the floor. "Lost something?"

"My engagement ring," she said, choking on the words. "I can't find it."

Sadie tried desperately to get control of herself, but her sobs continued in dry hiccups. Why did Reese have to come home just now?

"We'll find it, Sadie, so hush your crying." He peered under the stove, then reached his hand into the darkened slit between the stove and refrigerator. "I don't suppose you'd settle for an aluminum flip-top, would you?" he said, trying to coax a smile. "We seem to have an abundance of these." He offered the metal tab and attempted to slip it on her finger, but fresh tears welled up in her eyes. "Hey, it was just a joke."

"It isn't funny."

He pulled out his clean handkerchief and handed it to her. "Blow," he said. He gripped the metal strip at the bottom of the refrigerator, popping it loose. "Aha!" he shouted, reaching into the dark interior, then pulling out the diamond solitaire with his thumb and forefinger.

"You found it!" Sadie felt an enormous relief.

Reese reached for her hand. "Here you are," he said, trying to slip the ring onto her finger. "Back where it belongs."

A strange awkwardness came over Sadie. "No," she said, pulling back her hand. "I had to find it before I left—" She began to stammer. "I'm not—I mean, we've decided not—Jerry Don is—" She broke off in confusion, still refusing to accept the ring, which Reese continued to thrust in her direction.

"Sadie, what in the hell is going on?" Reese took her face between his hands and forced her to look at him. "I come home and find you bawling like a calf that's lost its mother and figure it's because you've lost your ring. But now you won't take the ring when I hand it to you, and you won't say anything that makes any sense."

Sadie couldn't bear his relentless gaze. It seemed as though he could see clear into her soul and discover every secret. She flung herself against his chest to hide her pain from him. "I can't talk about it," she whispered.

"Did you and Jerry Don have another fight? Is that it?"

She nodded.

"About his drinking?"

She didn't answer.

Reese swore under his breath. "Was he drunk when he left?"

"Not exactly drunk. But he'd had a lot."

"Where did he go?"

"I don't know. He was yelling something about Tascosa."

"Tascosa *again*? He's already been there twice in the past week." There was a long silence, and Sadie could feel the tension in Reese's body.

"He's been going back home a lot this spring, Reese. I think he's happier there. College has turned into too much of a grind for someone like Jerry Don. He'd rather party than study."

"Who wouldn't?" There was anger below the surface of Reese's words.

Sadie pulled herself from the loose coil of Reese's arms and pushed her hair away from her face. She gave Reese a shaky smile, trying to brighten their mood. "Thanks for finding the ring. When we get things straightened out, Jerry Don can give it back to me. He didn't mean to throw it."

"He threw it? I thought you dropped it."

Sadie reached out to pat his shoulder. "It's okay, Reese. He was so mad he didn't know what he was doing."

"Jerry Don should know if he hurts you, he's going to have to answer to me." He gripped Sadie's arm. "What did he do to you?"

"I'm not hurt, Reese, just a little upset. Can't we just forget it? I can't stand any more of this! First

Jerry Don is mad, then you're mad. Can't we please stop all this fighting?'' With that, Sadie buried her face in her hands and began to cry again.

''Shh,'' Reese said, pulling her back into his arms. ''I'm not angry with you, Sadie. Don't cry. Not on my account.'' He wiped away her tears, then rested his face against the top of her head. ''Now, then, everything's going to be okay.'' He rocked her gently in his arms, holding her close.

At length Sadie felt her taut muscles relax in the comfort of Reese's embrace, and she lifted her face to thank him. Their eyes met; their gazes lingered.

Reese flinched as though from some deep inner pain. ''Oh, Sadie,'' he whispered. ''I've tried not to—'' Breaking off the words, he lowered his face, searching for her lips. He whispered her name again and again as their mouths brushed. With one hand he caught her chin and tilted it while he supported the back of her neck with his other hand. His mouth descended, then opened to let his tongue brush her lips with light, slick strokes.

Sadie didn't understand the feelings that sprang to life in her. She knew only that Reese had suddenly become the center of a spinning universe and that she must cling to him or be hurled into space. She tightened her arms around him, her only security in a new and bewildering world of sensation. What could she do but respond in kind to this onslaught of unleashed desire? Her head fell back, her lips parted, and in a new-old ritual, her tongue hesitated, then flicked out to touch his.

He shuddered in her arms, pulling her down beside him as their tongues continued a sensuous mating dance—teasing, hiding, then quivering in delightful union.

Sadie had not known it was possible to kiss like this, with a breathless urgency that melted all resistance and sought even greater physical satisfaction. She tossed and moaned softly as every nerve ending sparked with excitement. Beside her, Reese groaned, then shifted her body beneath his, plundering her mouth while his hands moved upward from her hips, caressing her curves and valleys until he found his way to the buttons of her blouse. He fumbled with them, then tore at the catch of her bra until her breasts were loosened to his touch.

Sadie felt her nipples respond to his warmth as she became a blazing torch of desire. Reese tore his mouth from hers and tilted her so that her breasts thrust forward, easing his access. He lifted his hand to one rosy bud and stroked it until it blossomed with exquisite sensation, then turned to the other. Murmuring incoherent sounds of pleasure, Sadie shifted to lie above Reese, and now his mouth began a new plunder as he tugged and nipped at each swollen nipple.

He slipped his hands under her skirt to caress her hips, then moved them insistently around to her secret, womanly places. Sadie felt the heat raging in her body, a match to Reese's own. Her breath quickened, and her hand made a bashful virgin's journey down his body. When she touched the throbbing center of his being, Reese groaned aloud.

"Reese," she whispered, "I never felt like this before. I never knew what it was like to want to make love with someone." Shyly she kissed him. "I want to make love with you." She twisted in his arms and smiled down at him, starry-eyed with desire. It seemed right to be here in Reese's arms and experiencing these new feelings with him. She lifted his head and cradled it closer to her, offering him the pleasure of her sweetly aching breast.

Her words seemed to drive away the fog of passion that clouded his brain. A grim look came over his face, and she saw the muscle work at the corner of his jaw. "Sadie, I'm sorry," he said, scrambling into a sitting position. "This shouldn't have happened. I took advantage of you when you were upset." He averted his head and tried to get his breathing under control.

Sadie was confused. "But Reese," she protested. Her body was still clamoring for his touch. "I wanted you to do that." She reached out and let her finger trace the lines of his shoulder blades. "I didn't want you to stop." She sat up and buried her face against his back. "Kiss me like that again, Reese."

He half turned toward her and saw that her blouse was still unbuttoned, her breasts still exposed. "Oh, Sadie. Don't do this to me."

She stroked the hair at the nape of his neck. "Reese? Kiss me?"

"No, Sadie. You're just trying to get even with Jerry Don because you got in a fight with him. I'm not going to betray my best friend over a lovers' quarrel."

Sadie shook her head. "My fight with Jerry Don didn't have anything to do with what I was feeling for you, Reese."

"Listen, Sadie, I'm not just some poor jerk to fill a few idle moments of your spare time until Jerry Don whistles and you go running back to him. I'm a person, too, you know. I've got feelings of my own, or haven't you noticed?"

His angry words had a chilling effect on Sadie's desire, and she couldn't help taking a gibe at him. "As a matter of fact, you seemed to be having some pretty strong feelings for a few minutes there, so don't act like what happened between us had nothing to do with you."

"Damn it, Sadie," he sputtered, getting to his feet. "We were the victims of circumstance. So let it go, okay? It could happen to anybody."

Sadie was stunned. "Do you mean to say that this would have happened if I'd been any other reasonably attractive female or if you'd been any other reasonably attractive male? Is that all it meant to you? Just a few minutes of—of *lust*?"

"No, I didn't mean that." Reese took a deep, steadying breath and seemed to be searching for the right thing to say. "Look, the more we talk, the worse it gets." Reese obviously didn't know how to deal with the situation, and Sadie was glad to watch him squirm. Slowly she adjusted her bra and fastened it, then took her time rebuttoning her blouse. Finally she got to her feet and stood facing Reese.

"You blew it, Reese. I've never felt like that in my life before. I may never feel that way again. I've been engaged to Jerry Don for four years, and I've never let him touch me the way you did. I've never had the feelings for him that I had with you. I thought what happened between us just now was special. I was willing to trust you enough to give myself to you totally and completely. I'm sorry that to you it was nothing more than base animal instinct you could experience with just anybody, because it was a whole lot more than that to me." She drew a shaky breath but managed to hold back her tears. She was determined not to let Reese see how badly he'd hurt her. "You've taught me a good lesson, Reese Chandler. You've taken something wonderful and turned it into something ugly. I'll know better than to ever trust anybody else the way I trusted you." By the time she finished, Sadie's cheeks were scarlet with anger and humiliation. "I hope I never set eyes on you again as long as I live. You've made me feel cheap and dirty."

In one fluid motion she rushed into the living room and grabbed her books and car keys while Reese struggled to recover from her angry outburst. "Sadie," he protested, "wait. You don't understand. Let me explain."

But he was too late. She was flying down the steps to her car below.

Sadie rolled over onto her back and watched the play of light and shadow in the rustling leaves overhead. The flood of memories had drained her of all emotion, and she lay there, exhausted from the effort of experiencing anew the trauma of six years ago. At least Jerry Don had made it safely home to Tascosa, so she didn't have to feel guilt-ridden that their argument had precipitated his car wreck and ensuing death. He'd spent the night with his parents and started back to college early the next morning. It was on the return trip that the Thunderbird had spun off the road at high speed, and into a tree.

What would have happened if Jerry Don hadn't been killed? All these years Sadie had told herself they would have married and had a family. It was only by forcing her mind to remember honestly and painfully their last evening together that she began to wonder whether that was true. The doubt didn't take away her remorse over their parting argument, however, and she would have given anything for the opportunity to erase that event and relive the time. The worst memory of all was knowing that her final moments with Jerry Don had been spent in breaking off their engagement.

What might have happened if the news of Jerry Don's death hadn't erected an impenetrable wall between her and Reese? Even more tantalizing, what if she and Reese had made love that night? She had guessed right when she'd angrily exclaimed to Reese that she might never have those same passionate feelings for anyone else. She'd been young and naive then, but she'd known herself well enough to realize that what she'd experienced with Reese was special. There had been other men in Sadie's life since that time, but never anyone who could match that brief ecstasy with Reese—

Until now. And it was Reese himself who'd rekindled all that fiery passion during this past week. Last night at the class reunion, she'd been as eager for his touch as she'd been six years earlier. It was only maturity that now warned Sadie to be more cautious than she'd been before. She wasn't willing to let herself be hurt by Reese again. She would keep up her guard with him.

And yet . . . she had to acknowledge that even here in the shade of the cottonwood trees, all by herself, goose bumps raced up her spine at the memory of his kiss.

"So you're finally awake?" Sadie said to her mother, giving a cheerful smile as she carried in a lunch tray. "I thought you were going to sleep all afternoon."

"My goodness, I didn't know a little trip to church would be so exhausting," Nelda said, looking a trifle woebegone as she tried to sit up in bed. "I'm afraid I should have taken your advice and stayed home, Sadie. I believe I overdid it."

"Oh, you're probably just hungry. You fell asleep as soon as we got home, without eating a bite." Sadie helped her mother into the bathroom, then straightened the bedcovers and arranged the tray beside the rocking chair. "I brought you some fried chicken from the class reunion last night. It's Rose Alice's, and it's almost as good as her mother used to make."

Nelda sank into the rocker and took a few bites from her plate. "Did you make the spinach salad, Sadie? It's delicious."

"Fresh from your garden."

The women chatted for a while. When Nelda inquired about the reunion, Sadie told her *almost* everything. But she carefully censored any mention of Reese and their physical encounter.

"Did you hear that Al Peterson is retiring as high-school principal?" Nelda asked.

Sadie tensed. Her mother was leading up to something. "Yes, he was there to tell everyone goodbye. It was good to see him again."

"I don't believe the school board has hired anyone to take his place yet."

"That's what I heard." Sadie tried to keep her voice noncommittal.

"Well, then—" Nelda's hazel eyes brightened with anticipation "—that means there's a principal's job open right here in Tascosa. Now that you've finished your administrator's certification, it would be a perfect job for you."

"Now, Mom, don't let your imagination run away with you. Sure, I said someday I want to get a principal's job and settle down, but I never said anything about coming back to Tascosa. I don't fit in here anymore."

"But, Sadie—"

"Mom, please don't get your hopes up. I'm not going to apply for Mr. Peterson's job. Can't you understand I don't want to come back to Tascosa?"

"But why, Sadie? The people who love you are all here. This is where you belong." Nelda's chin had that same determined tilt. She wasn't going to give up easily.

"This is where I *used* to belong, Mom. Not anymore. What am I supposed to talk about when you and Wynona start discussing peach preserves and crocheted afghans? And who's going to talk to me about my work—the education reforms, and school curriculum, and 'no-pass no-play'? There's nobody here who speaks the same language I do, Mom."

"That isn't true, Sadie. I may not know about all those things, but the teachers at school do. And we had a lawsuit last fall when a student flunked chemistry and got put off the football team. I believe everybody in town can talk about the 'no-pass no-play' rules."

There was no point in trying to deal with her mother's obstinacy, Sadie realized. "How's the fried chicken?"

"Never mind the fried chicken. It's your future we're talking about, daughter."

Sadie's head flew up. When Nelda used that tone and called her "daughter," Sadie knew her mother had her dander up. She'd need to be more conciliatory. "Mom, that's my point. I don't have a future in Tascosa. This is no place for a single person to live. Everybody else is married and has kids, and it makes me feel like a fifth wheel."

"Reese manages just fine, and he's single."

"Yes, but they say he's made a lot of single friends in nearby towns. He does his socializing with people in Hereford and Canyon."

"He wouldn't have to do that if you were here in Tascosa." Nelda wiped her mouth on her paper napkin and shoved her plate aside. "If you came home, you and Reese would probably get married."

"I know that's what you've got in your mind, Mom, but your scheme isn't going to work, so you might as well forget it. I don't want to get married to somebody just because he's the only available man in town and I'm the only available female, and we've ended up stuck with each other for lack of any other choice. That isn't the future I want for myself, thank you very much."

"I'm your mother, Sadie. Don't use that tone of voice with me."

Sadie straightened the medicine bottles on the nightstand and tried to hold on to her patience. "You're also supposed to be my friend, Mom. Can't you understand? It just won't work. I don't want to come back to Tascosa. There are too many painful memories for me here. You want me to be happy, don't you?"

"Of course I do, Sadie. That's why I want you to come home. Anyone who knows you can tell you aren't happy now. You're tired of your job. You said so yourself. You're too thin and edgy, and no matter how big a smile you plaster on your face, you can't hide the sadness in your eyes from me." Nelda eased herself from the rocker and moved toward the bed, pushing her dusty-red hair from her forehead. "I'm worn-out," she said. "I'm going to rest for a while. Let me know when Reese comes by. I want to talk to him."

"He didn't say anything to me about coming back. He's going to have to work late to make up the time he lost taking us to church this morning."

"He'll come by. He said he would. Even if it's late, I want you to wake me."

"But why?"

"Because he's on the school board. I want to find out if they've interviewed anybody for Al Peterson's job."

"Mom, you didn't listen to a word I said, did you?"

Nelda curled into a comfortable ball, her back to Sadie. "Why don't you make a batch of chocolate-chip cookies, dear? They were always Reese's favorite."

Chapter Seven

Sadie removed the last sheet of cookies from the oven and set them aside to cool while she finished washing up. The kitchen was full of the tantalizing aroma of chocolate and brown sugar, and Sadie realized how rarely she baked in Austin. No wonder her apartment seemed more like a motel than a home, when there was never the comforting fragrance of food cooking. Tonight she'd baked the chocolate-chip cookies her mother had insisted upon, hoping that by giving in to a small request, she could head off further battles about the big one she must refuse. Somehow her mother would have to accept the fact that Sadie was not going to come back to Tascosa to live. If baking cookies made that fact more palatable, Sadie would bake cookies every day.

She'd just folded the dish towel when she heard Reese's pickup coming down the road. Quickly Sadie poured a glass of cold milk, arranged a plate of cookies on a tray, and went to rouse her mother. "I'm going to make myself scarce while you and Reese are visiting," she said firmly, then left her mother's bedroom. She was just making her escape through the kitchen door when she heard Reese's knock at the front. "Come on in," she called over her shoulder. "Mom's awake and says she wants to see you."

Sadie hurried down to the grove of cottonwood trees, which were heady now with the nighttime scent of honeysuckle. Maybe it was rude of her to disappear this way, but she didn't intend to get into any more arguments with anyone today; and arguments were definitely brewing. Her coming back to Tascosa had stirred up everything and reopened all the old wounds that were better left alone, so it would be a long time before she returned to Tascosa again. Not even Christmas would bring her back this year. She'd try to talk her mother into a Caribbean cruise instead.

Sadie threw herself onto the ground in a heap of dejection. Right now she felt trapped by circumstances, held hostage by a simple plaster cast. She'd been here for more than a week now, and she needed to get back to her life in Austin. Her mother had been coming along pretty well until today, when the trip to church had proved too much for her. Tomorrow Sadie would call the doctor to see whether her mother could travel. If so, she'd take her mother back to Austin. If Sadie had to stay in Tascosa much longer, she thought she'd start screaming from boredom and frustration. And a change of scene would be good for her mother, too.

Sadie realized her thoughts were whirling crazily, leapfrogging from one problem to another without anything being resolved. She needed to get back to work and focus her mind on something tangible. In the meantime, though, she was going to have to find a way to deal with the emotional stress of this forced journey to the past.

The back door slammed, and Sadie edged over near a lilac bush. In the darkness Reese probably wouldn't be able to see her, and maybe he'd go on his way. She had enough emotional baggage of her own to deal with tonight. She wasn't up to coping with more of that enigmatic anger he'd displayed at the cemetery this morning.

"Sadie?"

She hunkered into a ball and didn't respond.

"You're not playing hide-and-seek, are you?" She could hear his footfalls drawing nearer the grove. "I brought something for you, Sadie. Found it in a wheat field this afternoon."

Curiosity piqued her, but still she didn't answer.

"Last chance," he said.

Sadie could tell he'd stopped moving and was waiting for her. He wasn't yet sure whether she was here, and must be wondering where else she might be.

"If a rattlesnake gets it, you'll only have yourself to blame."

Sadie couldn't hold back her laughter. "You win, again," she said. He knew all her characteristics too well—even her curiosity. "What did you bring me?"

Reese walked toward the sound of her voice, whistling softly in the moonlight. "A baby rabbit," he said. "A hawk got its mother. I think it's big enough to live if you'll mother it for a few days."

Sadie scrambled to her feet. "Oh, Reese," she said, taking the soft, furry ball from him and cuddling it against her breast. "How precious." She stroked the warm fur and felt the bunny's damp nose against her fingers. "Poor baby," she crooned.

"I've never known you to turn down a stray animal yet," Reese said. "I figured you wouldn't want me to leave it for the hawk to get on his next pass over the field."

"I'll have to rig up some kind of cage for it," Sadie said, all her attention on the tiny, trembling creature. "Otherwise a stray dog or something will kill it."

"Or it'll eat everything in your mother's vegetable garden," Reese said, chuckling. "I'll bring over some wire mesh tomorrow and help you build a hutch."

"What am I going to do with it tonight, though?"

"I left a big cardboard box by your kitchen door."

Sadie felt his gaze on her. "I'm glad you brought the rabbit to me," she said. "It's so helpless, isn't it?" She continued to stroke the animal, and eventually its little heart quit pounding so furiously. Sadie sat down on the grass and Reese settled beside her.

"What a day!" he said, sounding weary.

"Did you have to work hard?"

"We moved a lot of wheat this afternoon. We completely finished that northwest quarter-section."

"How much is left?" The rabbit was asleep, and Sadie nestled it in her lap.

"We're down to the last quarter-section. It's not ready yet, though. Looks like we're going to have a break to do something else besides run the combine for a couple of days. I think I'm going to work the cattle tomorrow. I want to get off the tractor and onto a horse again."

"That sounds great," Sadie said. "I'd love to go horseback riding again."

Reese shot Sadie a glance in the moonlight. "I've been so busy working I didn't think about what you were doing all day. I guess time passes a lot slower when you're nursing an invalid. During harvest there aren't enough hours in the day for me."

"Wynona usually drops by in the afternoon while Mom is taking her nap. It helps to get to visit with her and play with the kids." Sadie smiled. "They give me a real workout. They take more energy than a trip to the gym."

They continued to chat about ranch chores and the harvest—topics that were noncontroversial. At times like this, Sadie reflected, she and Reese could talk so easily, laugh at the same things. It was only when the conversation skirted old times that they began to knot up and feel tense. An hour passed, then another, and the moon was high in the sky.

Finally Reese yawned. "I've got to get myself home to bed," he said. "Your mother sent me down here with a job to do, and you've managed to change the subject every time I got near it. I give up, Sadie. I'll try again tomorrow."

"Thanks for the reprieve," she answered, getting to her feet.

"Don't call it a reprieve," Reese replied. "Call it a warning." He put his hand loosely across her shoulders and walked her to the kitchen door. "By the way," he said, "thanks for the cookies. Chocolate-chip cookies were always my favorite."

The light from the kitchen exposed the wry grin on Sadie's face. "That's what Mom remembered," she said. "You can call that a warning, too."

Sadie was throwing an easy pitch to Wynona's son Aaron the following afternoon when dust clouds and the hum of a truck engine announced Reese's arrival. The children all ran to meet him while Sadie went inside to get him a glass of iced tea.

"Thanks," he said, half draining the glass with one swallow. "It's hot today." Rumpling Aaron's blond hair, he said, "Come along, Aaron. We've got work to do."

Sadie and Wynona watched Reese hand several short boards to Aaron, a hammer to Biff and a bag of nails to Becka. He herded the children around to the shady side of the house, then unrolled a coil of wire mesh, measured it, and cut it with tin snips. In no time, everyone was busy holding or pounding something in a community effort to build a sturdy cage for the baby rabbit, which the children had named Sniffles.

"We need a dish for his water," Biff said when the project was complete and Sniffles had been installed in his new home.

"And lettuce for him to eat." Aaron looked at Sadie. "Do you have any?"

"Let's go down to the garden and see." Sadie took Aaron's hand in hers. "Wynona, see if you can find Biff a bowl for water. There ought to be something he can use in the kitchen cupboard."

Sadie took Aaron to the garden plot and showed him the rows of lettuce, spinach, radishes, and carrots. "Sniffles can eat any of these," she said. "Which one do you want to give him today?"

With a look of boyish mischief, Aaron quickly tugged vegetables from each row. "One of each!" He ran on his sturdy little legs, laughing at Sadie over his shoulder. "Tricked you!" he shouted in glee. He threw himself into his mother's arms, out of breath. "I tricked Sadie," he said, still laughing as she caught up with him.

Sadie sat down on a lawn chair and gave Aaron a mock scolding. "You're a typical male, all right," she said, wagging her finger at him. "That's just the kind of stunt Reese and Jerry Don pulled when they were little boys. I bet your father did the same thing, too."

Aaron flung himself on the grass and gleefully kicked his feet like a beetle trying to get upright again. He was enjoying his moment of triumph. "I tricked you, I tricked you!"

Sadie got down on her hands and knees beside him, then yanked up his T-shirt and began to tickle him until he screamed with delightful abandon. "Now who's getting tricked?" she said, tickling him some more, then rubbing handfuls of grass under his shirt.

Aaron thrashed and kicked until everyone wanted to be in a tickle fight. Wynona moved her chair a safe distance away while Reese and Sadie roughhoused with the three older children.

"That's enough," Sadie said at last, breathless from exertion.

Aaron couldn't quit without one final act. He sneaked toward Sadie's feet and pulled off her sandal, then tickled the sole of her foot. When she grabbed him and threatened to toss him into the air, he grinned at her in pure devilment.

"You monkey," she said, laughing. "You win. You got the last blow, didn't you?" She gave him a hug. "Go give some of that lettuce to Sniffles," she said, then turned to smile at Wynona and Reese. "Isn't it funny that all little boys have that same mischievous expression when they've gotten the best of grown-ups? I bet I've seen that look a thousand times—most of the time on Jerry Don's face."

Reese and Wynona exchanged uneasy glances. Reese cleared his throat. "And mine. And Tom's. And yours, too, Sadie. You and Wynona used to be capable of some pretty devilish grins yourselves, if the truth be told."

Melanie let out a yell. "Oh-oh," Wynona said. "I think this imp needs her diaper changed. Come on, kids," she called. "We're out of diapers. We've got to go home. Tell Sniffles goodbye for now."

"Aw, Mom, do we have to?" There were protests from the children, who were having too much fun to leave, but Wynona was firm.

"Now, remember, Sadie, you're coming for supper with us tomorrow night. Tom wants to see you again before you leave. You come, too, Reese. Seven o'clock." With the usual flurry of goodbyes, Wynona rounded up the children and made a hasty departure.

"What's this about your leaving?" Reese asked after they'd gone.

"The doctor came by this morning. He says Mom is doing fine, but she's malingering, trying to keep me here." Sadie brushed blades of grass from her legs. "I tried to talk her into going back to Austin with me, but she turned me down. The doctor says for me to go on without her, because it will be better for me to leave before she gets too dependent on me." Sadie realized her explanation was becoming defensive and stopped talking.

A controlled expression had come over Reese's face, as though he didn't want Sadie to know what he was thinking. "So when are you leaving?" he asked.

"Day after tomorrow. I'll try to get an early start so I won't have to be on the highway during the worst heat of the afternoon."

"Yeah, sure. Good idea. It's supposed to get even hotter the rest of the week." Reese began to gather up his tools, so Sadie helped him. They carried everything around to his pickup in the driveway. "What are you going to do with Sniffles when you leave?" he asked.

"Give him to Wynona's children." There was a sudden emptiness inside Sadie, but it was the only possible answer. She couldn't keep a rabbit in her Austin apartment, and her mother certainly didn't need an animal to take care of.

"Right." He gave her a searching glance. "So tomorrow is your last day, then?"

Sadie nodded. Why did she feel like weeping?

Reese pushed his dark hair back from his forehead. The sun had bronzed him during the long hours outdoors, and in the vee of his open shirt, Sadie could see curly hair against smooth, dark skin.

"Okay if I stop by this evening after we finish with the cattle?" he asked. "We took a break during the heat of the day, but it's time to get started again. I still have that unfinished errand for your mom. Maybe we can talk about it tonight."

Sadie shrugged. "It's not going to change anything, but if it'll make you feel better to try, okay. Would you like to come for supper?"

Reese shook his head. "It'll be too late. Don't expect me before nine-thirty or ten." He lifted himself into the cab of the truck and smiled down at her. "I don't mind if you save me a few chocolate-chip cookies, though."

Sadie had taken a long soak in a tub full of bubbles, then put on the flowing green gauze outfit that she knew made her eyes sparkle. She'd twisted her hair into a loose coil at the top of her head, with tendrils at her temples and the nape of her neck. She dug through her traveling kit until she found green enameled earrings in the shape of a flower and, after checking herself in the mirror, dabbed scent of lily-of-the-valley behind her ears. She'd just finished dressing when she heard Reese's knock on the front door. Nine-fifteen. He was early.

She started toward the living room, then hurried back. There was a lace-trimmed handkerchief in her dresser drawer, left behind years before. She put it in her pocket, just in case. If their conversation made her weepy tonight, she at least wanted to have her own handkerchief.

"Come in," she said, opening the door for Reese.

He took off his cowboy hat, stepped inside, and stood there looking at her while his hands automatically rotated the hat along its inside band. Nervously he cleared his throat. Then he grinned at her. "I was looking for Sadie McClure," he said, "but I'll be happy to settle for you. Are you one of those movie actresses who just happened to be in town?"

Sadie's lips formed a dazzling smile. It was the first time since she'd been in Tascosa that she felt she was at her best. "You don't look so bad yourself," she replied. Reese was wearing khaki slacks instead of his usual jeans, and a fresh white shirt, that made his skin look even more tanned than it was. Tonight his eyes had a friendly expression, and there was a smile lurking at the corners of his mouth. Maybe she wouldn't need her handkerchief, after all. "Can I get you something cold to drink?"

"That sounds good. It's still pretty hot outside." He followed her into the kitchen.

"What'll it be," Sadie asked, "iced tea or lemonade?"

"Frozen lemonade or homemade?"

Sadie filled tall glasses with ice. "My goodness, you don't think I'd dare to serve store-bought lemonade to anyone in Tascosa, do you? I squeezed the lemons myself. Hope I put in enough sugar," she added, pouring from an etched-glass pitcher.

Reese took a tentative taste and pronounced the lemonade delicious, then went to sit down at the kitchen table.

Sadie hesitated. If they had their discussion here, her mother might overhear them. "Let's go outside," she said. She'd just as soon have the protection of darkness, anyway, rather than the bright kitchen light that revealed her every emotion.

They sat on the porch steps while they sipped their lemonade, their shoulders brushing. The comfortable silence began to lengthen. Reese was here for a purpose, and they both knew what it was.

"Well, Reese, what's on your mind?"

He shoved his empty lemonade glass across the porch, out of the way. "I guess you have a pretty good idea of what your mom wants, Sadie."

"Her hints haven't been very subtle. She seems to have my life all planned out for me. Come back to Tascosa, take over Mr. Peterson's job as high-school principal, and marry you." Sadie's voice was flat. "She didn't tell me yet where she plans for me to live, though. Are we supposed to stay here with her or take her with us to live at your place?"

Reese's hand touched the back of Sadie's neck and toyed with the stray tendrils there. "I don't think she's planned that far ahead yet."

"Why did you let her drag you into this, Reese? I'm tired of fighting with you. Let's don't get into another argument, okay?" Sadie leaned her head against Reese's shoulder and laid one hand against his bare arm. "I'm so much happier when we can be friends, and we won't be if you take Mom's side in this."

"I'm not taking her side, Sadie. She asked me to talk to you about applying for Mr. Peterson's job, that's all."

Sadie tried to control her impatience. "Okay, tell me about the job, then. I'll listen, and then you can tell her I said no."

"About ten people have applied for the job so far, and we're expecting some more applications. There's nobody in Tascosa who's qualified, though, and the school board would prefer to hire a native. They'd like to hire somebody who'll be around for a long time instead of someone who'll move on to a bigger school district in a couple of years."

"What about Mr. Jones, the math teacher? I thought he'd started working on an administrator's certificate several years ago."

"He did, but he never finished his course work. I think he lost interest."

"It might be good for Tascosa to bring in somebody from the outside. The winds of change and all that."

"Maybe so, if we could find the right outsider. It's going to take somebody who understands the Texas Panhandle, though. Folks here are different. They're independent and self-reliant, and they give a lot to their schools. Expect a lot, too. Parents here are perfectly happy if their kids go to college at Texas Tech, but they want the high school to prepare them just as well as it would for Harvard and Stanford."

Sadie reached for Reese's hand and gave it a gentle squeeze. "I think that's the longest speech I've ever heard you make, Reese."

"Guess that comes from serving on the school board for four years. I've sure learned a lot about running schools so kids get a good education and the taxpayers get their money's worth." He gave her an abashed grin in the moonlight. "Didn't mean to get on my soapbox, though. I think I've been preaching to the converted, and that's not what your mother asked me to do."

"Don't get off your soapbox on my account. I was hoping we could change the subject."

Reese lifted her fingers to his lips and brushed them with a kiss. "You smell so nice it's hard to keep my mind on any subject," he said with a new hoarseness in his voice. "If I hadn't made that promise to your mother—"

Sadie turned to face him, her fingers still clasped next to his lips. She stroked his cheek with her thumb and said softly, "Reese, tomorrow is my last day in Tascosa. Then I'm going back to Austin, to my job and to my life there. That's what's right for me. I don't belong here anymore, and I'd be unhappy if I stayed. Please try to help Mom understand that, won't you?"

Stray moonbeams of light played across Reese's face and reflected off his eyes. "Are you sure, Sadie?"

"I'm sure, Reese. I can't escape from Jerry Don's ghost here. How could I work in the high school every day, with those glass cases full of trophies with his name on them? And every classroom where he used to sit, with memories of the way he'd tease Miss Ledbetter or argue with Mr. Deavers? Or go to football games and remember him quarterbacking the team? Why does Mom want to put me through that kind of ordeal?''

"Don't you think it's the same for the rest of us?'' Reese held Sadie's face between his hands so she couldn't avert her gaze from his.

"Is it?'' she asked, almost surprised at the notion. "Then, God help us all.''

The pain in her voice seemed to anger Reese. "We all have our memories, Sadie. You're not the only one who hurts, or wants to run away from them.''

"Maybe not,'' she said, stung by his criticism. "But maybe I'm the only one who managed to do it. Why drag me back when I've made my escape from all that pain? Is it so noble and adult to wallow in misery? If you want to escape Jerry Don's ghost and can't find a way to do it, why make me feel guilty because I did?''

"Nobody wants you to come back to Tascosa if you don't want to, Sadie. Not even your mother. She thinks you're unhappy in Austin, and she's worried about you. That's why she wants you to come home.''

Sadie jumped to her feet. "Well, she's wrong! I have a good life in Austin. I've never been happier.'' Tears rushed to her eyes, and she felt them burn a scalding trickle down her cheeks.

Reese rose slowly to his feet, as though a sudden movement might send her scurrying away. "It's okay,

Sadie," he said gently. "You've made your point. I believe you." He reached into his hip pocket and pulled out a handkerchief.

"Never mind," she said, thrusting a hand into her own pocket. "I expected this to happen." She pulled out the lace-trimmed handkerchief and dabbed at her eyes.

Reese uttered a rueful chuckle. "It's a hell of a note when we both come prepared for you to cry, Sadie. No wonder you don't want to come back to Tascosa. You were meant for laughter, not tears." He took a step toward her and opened his arms. "I'm sorry, sweetheart. Forget the whole damned thing. It's the last time I'll let your mother talk me into doing something that's against my better judgment."

Sadie stepped into his arms and felt them tighten about her. The warmth and security she'd hungered for were right here. He wasn't going to be angry with her again, after all. She drew a shaky breath and lifted her face for his kiss. The future would have to wait.

Chapter Eight

Sadie wakened the next morning to the sounds and smells of perking coffee and sizzling bacon. What was her mother doing in the kitchen at this hour? It wasn't yet six o'clock. Sadie rolled over in bed, puzzled at the banging of pans in the kitchen, which was soon followed by steps back and forth in the hallway to a whistled rendition of "Ladies Love Outlaws," an old country-and-western song that had been popular when she was in high school.

Sadie sat bolt upright in bed just as Reese walked through the doorway, a breakfast tray in his hands.

"Good morning," he said, grinning down at her. "I let myself in with a key. Since this is your last day in Tascosa, I figured we ought to make the most of it."

He found a spot for the tray on the bedside stand and put it down. "Well?" he said, apparently amused at her stunned silence.

"Well, this is—very nice," she stammered. She looked at the tray. Hot coffee steamed from a mug, and she saw an omelet, crisp bacon, orange juice, and buttered toast. But the thing that caught Sadie's eye first and last was a bud vase containing yellow roses and blue morning glories freshly cut from the garden. She reached out to touch the velvety petals of the rosebuds. "You think of everything, don't you?" she said in a voice that had suddenly become breathless.

There was a mischievous glint in his eyes. "For today, yes, I've thought of everything. I've already taken breakfast to your mom. As soon as you've eaten and dressed, you're going with me to the ranch."

"Reese, I can't. This is my last day in Tascosa. I can't leave Mom alone."

"She's not going to be alone, and she wants you to go. Al Peterson is going to come spend the morning with her, and I'll bring you back right after lunch so you can spend the rest of the day with her."

"Mr. Peterson? The high-school principal? Why him?"

"Don't be so suspicious. They're not going to gang up on you to apply for Al's job. He's been lonely since his wife died, and he said he could bring his paperwork over here this morning. The company will be good for both of them."

It gave Sadie a weird feeling to think of her mother enjoying the "company" of Al Peterson in his new role as marriageable widower. Her mother had always said no one could take the place of Sadie's father, and as far as Sadie knew, she'd never given another man a serious glance. It was as though Sadie's mother had remained married to her father's memory, in the same way that Sadie had been permanently bound to Jerry Don's memory. "Is something going on that nobody's mentioned to me?"

"Not yet." Reese gave her an enigmatic smile. "Now, rise and shine, before your breakfast gets cold. The day is getting away from us." Reese reached to pull the sheet from Sadie's shoulders and hurry her from the bed.

"Don't," she said, her face flaming crimson as she held the sheet tightly with both hands.

Reese gave her a calculating look, then laughed. "Was it too hot to sleep in a nightgown last night?" He bent his head to lightly brush her lips with his, then flicked his tongue over her bottom lip. "It's even hotter today," he whispered. "By noon it's supposed to be 106 degrees. So dress accordingly."

He moved his hand from her shoulder to her arm, then to the sheet clutched in her hands. For a spine-tingling moment he caressed her with his palm, and Sadie felt her nipple throb and harden to his touch.

She let go of the sheet.

Reese knelt to bury his face in the softness of her breasts, his breath warm as it fluttered against her sensitive nerve endings and sent goose bumps of excitement racing up her spine. Sadie lifted one hand over her head, then twisted slightly, mutely inviting him to take his pleasure in her eager flesh. His breath came faster, and she could see that his eyes were smoky with desire. She trembled with anticipation as he cupped her breast and lifted it to his lips. For a moment he held it there. Then he began to tease her with his tongue, licking and stroking at the dark rose outer circle. Sadie thrust upward against him, and he closed his mouth with full pressure on her nipple, sending her into a frenzy of wanting more. She twisted again, drawing him to her other breast, and moaned as it, too, pulsed and throbbed to his sensual attentions.

Desire sent a roaring through her ears, and she felt a melting heat. Her head fell back, and she abandoned herself to wave after wave of ecstasy. Her mind was so cloudy with passion that she didn't hear her mother's voice calling her. Reese broke away.

"Sadie, someone's knocking at the door," Nelda repeated. "Can you answer it?"

"I'll be there in just a minute, Mom." Sadie looked down at herself and smiled shyly. The blue veins of her breasts contrasted with her ivory skin, and her nipples were still swollen and sweetly aching from Reese's plundering mouth. "But not like this," she whispered against his ear.

"I'll answer it," he replied. "It's probably Al Peterson. I'll visit with him while you get dressed."

"What about this wonderful breakfast you cooked for me?"

"You had your choice," Reese said, rising to go and answer the door. "And like a sensible woman, you chose a cold breakfast and a warm kiss instead of vice versa."

"I'm certainly curious about your plans for lunch," Sadie answered.

Reese grinned. "Lunch will definitely be a heartier meal. The day is only beginning."

"'Bout time you showed up!" called Dwaine Pickens, a ranch hand who was already on horseback when Reese and Sadie pulled through the gateway. "It's almost seven o'clock. The day's half gone."

Reese waved as he parked his pickup truck on the tire-rutted path that served as a road. "Blame it on Sadie," he answered. "She's gotten lazy living in the city and doesn't jump out of bed at five o'clock like we do."

Sadie clambered down from the truck, waving at Dwaine and a second cowboy, Buster Wells. Both men were as sun bronzed as Reese himself, and lean-legged with broad shoulders and sinewy arms.

Sadie looked at the sorrel-colored quarter horse with the black mane that had been saddled for her use and wondered if she could keep up with the men this morning. They practically slept on horseback, and she hadn't been on a horse in six years.

She took a deep breath and lifted her foot into the stirrup, then grabbed the saddle horn and propelled herself into the saddle. She turned toward Reese and smiled. She hadn't forgotten how to mount, after all. What she'd forgotten was the sense of exhilaration of being on horseback. She leaned forward and stroked behind the horse's ear. "Good girl," she whispered. "What's her name?"

"Sarah Jane."

Sadie gave Reese a surprised look. "That's what you used to call me in elementary school."

"Seemed like the right name for her. She's like you were then—a little ornery and headstrong, but feisty and lovable." Reese eased gracefully into the saddle of his own horse, a dark chestnut stallion, and checked the hemp lariat coiled around the saddle horn. Without glancing in Sadie's direction, he asked, "Does she look familiar to you?"

"The black mane reminds me of College Bound, the quarter horse Daddy gave me for my birthday when we were in high school."

Reese nodded. "Sarah Jane is College Bound's daughter."

When Sadie would have asked a dozen questions about how Reese had come into ownership of a filly born to a particular horse sold long ago, he evaded her by signaling to the men. "Let's get a move on before it gets any hotter. We've got two hundred head of cattle to move to new pasture before noon."

Before long the sun had sent rivulets of perspiration down Sadie's forehead and shoulders, and she welcomed the broad-brimmed cowboy hat lent by Dwaine to keep her face in shadow. Sarah Jane was surefooted and self-directed, so accustomed to ranch tasks that she needed only the merest nudge from Sadie for guidance. Unlike the horse, Sadie found that she herself had to watch carefully and wait for instructions in order to know how to help the men move the cattle.

It became her job to ride alongside the single file of cattle, shouting over their petulant moos and bawlings to keep them moving, or whacking them on the rump with the brim of her hat to keep them from bunching up again. "Stupid cow!" she muttered, waiting for the dogs to come and nip at the hooves of an unusually stubborn heifer. "Don't you know there's good green grass in that new pasture? Why do you want to stay behind where there's nothing but overgrazed brown stubble?"

Reese had ridden up beside Sadie, but she hadn't heard him over the noise made by the cattle. "Cows are like some people," he said, cutting his horse in behind the cow and nudging it reluctantly forward. "Scared to risk something new, even when they'll be better off for it."

Sadie turned to look at him, but his expression was unreadable. "Surely you aren't talking about me?" she asked. "I'm the one who left Tascosa to see what the rest of the world was like."

"You're the one who left," Reese said softly. "But you're more tied to Tascosa's past than any of us who stayed here. The rest of us have found green, fresh pasture. You're still bawling because you want to keep feeding yourself on dead grass."

Sadie wasn't sure which emotion she felt most with his accusation. "I wouldn't say *you* have anything to brag about. You're living alone, doing the same thing you've always done—running a ranch. Where's the wonderful green pasture in *your* life, Reese? Where are the wife and kids you always wanted?"

"Just because things don't turn out the way you thought they would when you were eighteen doesn't mean life is empty and not worth living. At least *I'm* happy, Sadie. And that's more than you can say for yourself."

"How can I be happy, ever?" she said, the words surprised from her lips before her mind could censor them. "I never got a chance to make things right with Jerry Don."

Reese gave Sadie a hard look, then glanced at the cow he was trying to herd toward new pasture over its bellowing protests. With a twisted smile he cut his horse aside, and the cow scampered out of the way. He flapped it with his hat and it went scurrying away from the line toward its old familiar pasture.

"Why did you do that?" Sadie asked, puzzled. This had something to do with her, but she wasn't sure what.

"Let it go. If it wants to starve itself to death on empty fodder, so be it."

Sadie watched as the confused cow tried to move in the opposite direction from the others. "Reese, go get it," she said. "Don't let the cow starve because you're frustrated with me."

"I'm not punishing the cow," he answered sharply. "The cow is making its own choice. It can gnaw on something that's dead, or it can make the effort to find something new. This is a free country, even for cows." He formed a noose with his lariat, tossed it toward another cow, and pulled it into the gap left by the one that had stumbled backward to the old pasture. His shirt was streaked with sweat, and when he'd re-coiled the rope, he wiped his face with a dark bandana. Before he rode away, he said, "You know, Sadie, sometimes I think we should've buried you in that grave with Jerry Don. It would probably have been a kindness to you."

The morning passed quickly, so busy were they with the constant activity of moving two hundred head of recalcitrant, dull-witted cattle. Sadie's post on the sidelines gave her plenty of opportunity to watch the men, who were so accustomed to working together that they kept perfect rhythm by some invisible means of communication. There were no wasted motions as they moved down the line of cattle, urging and coaxing, expert and graceful with the task at hand.

Sadie tilted her cowboy hat and wiped her face with a bandana. She'd gotten separated from the men and was a short distance away from them, on the opposite side of the line of moving cattle. Across the way she saw Reese, upright and square-shouldered, his head tilted at a cocky angle. No question about it: physically, she felt only one thing for Reese, and that was desire. Even now, at this distance, she wanted to reach out and touch him, stroke the thick hair at the nape of his neck, trace her fingernail across the faint stubble of his beard.

What's happening to me? she wondered. Thirty minutes ago Reese and I exchanged angry words, yet all I can think about is getting him alone to myself and throwing myself into his arms. When he's kissing me, nothing else seems to matter—not the past, not Jerry Don, not the future. It's the present that's desperately real, and everything else is blotted out. Sadie held the reins lightly in one hand and glanced to see what Reese was doing. His horse, too, had stopped.

Sadie realized that Reese was watching her, with his gaze traveling down her body. Caught in the act, he tilted the brim of his cowboy hat at a raffish angle and gave her a lopsided grin. "Almost lunchtime," he called. "Anybody getting hungry?"

Dwaine and Buster decided to go into town for lunch so they could eat in air-conditioned comfort. They usually took a long break at midday, then returned for another five or six hours of work when the afternoon breeze and lengthening shadows made the heat bearable.

"Y'all going to join us?" Dwaine asked.

Reese shook his head. "Not today. We'll have a quick bite to eat and then Sadie's got to get back home to her mother." He closed the gate to the cross fence, blocking any exit for the cattle now grazing on fresh pasture. "We've finished here, and the wheat in the last field isn't ready for the combine yet. You guys might as well take the rest of the day off."

Dwaine and Buster exchanged sly smiles. "You bet. You want us to meet you at the house in the morning, or out in the field?"

"At the house. We can decide where we'll go from there."

The cowboys turned their horses to leave. "What about that heifer you left at the old pasture?" Buster called over his shoulder.

Reese muttered an oath. "She doesn't know what she wants or what's good for her. See if you can load her in the stock trailer and haul her to the barn. I'll hand-feed her for a few days and see if she'll straighten out." He gave Sadie a devilish grin. "If that doesn't work, I'll haul her to the cattle auction and sell her to the highest bidder. She'll make a lot of nice sirloin steaks for somebody's table if she doesn't get her act together."

The cowboys rode away laughing, but Sadie turned to Reese in horror. "Reese, you wouldn't!"

There was an unexpected harshness in his voice. "Maybe not, but I ought to. That would be better than letting her starve herself to death one slow day at a time. She's in a barren field with no life-support system. She can't stay there, but she won't let herself move forward with the other cattle. What can you do with a cow that's so confused it's gone loco?''

''Are you sure you're talking about that cow?''

Reese refused to meet her glance. ''I've brought the makings for a picnic lunch,'' he said. ''Let's ride down to the creek bed and build a fire to roast our hot dogs. I don't know about you, but I'm getting pretty hungry.''

''Yeah. Me, too,'' Sadie answered with a catch in her throat. ''It's been a long time since breakfast.''

Reese built a small fire with kindling, then added larger pieces broken from dead limbs of cottonwood trees that lined the creek bed. Before turning the horses loose to drink from the shallow creek, he'd removed a saddle blanket and spread it under the trees. Sadie lay on her back and stared up at the brilliant blue sky, listening to the peaceful sounds of nature.

''Coffee?'' Reese asked, pouring from a thermos. ''I can promise you it's strong.''

Sadie took the plastic cup and sat up to sip the scalding coffee. Though she was tired and sweat soaked, it was a good, healthy feeling resulting from the morning's sunshine, fresh air, and exercise. It was wonderful to be outdoors again, instead of being cooped up in the house all day. Or in an office.

She thought of returning to Austin the following day and for the first time felt a sense of dread about going back. Her ''office'' was a tiny cubicle about seven feet square, with no window. She'd always told herself it didn't matter about her office because she spent so little time in it anyway. Usually she was on the road, traveling from school to school. She took another sip of coffee and tilted back her head to gaze at the sky. She would miss its beauty in her windowless cubicle.

"Is the fire ready for the hot dogs?" she asked.

"Almost. It's burning a little too high right now, but it won't be long until the coals are white-hot and perfect."

"What else do we have?"

"Nothing fancy. Chips and a can of pork and beans. Ripe peaches and cherries from Wynona's orchard. Some marshmallows."

Sadie grinned. "Marshmallows toasted over a fire? Heavens, that certainly brings back old times. I don't think I've had any since we graduated from college."

"That's the bad part about growing up. The treats of childhood get left behind." Reese finished his coffee and got up to stoke the fire. "Remember how we loved licorice shoestrings and caramel suckers when we were kids?"

Sadie rubbed her stomach and laughed. "We couldn't see a movie without them. It's a wonder our teeth didn't rot." Sadie set aside her cup and stretched out on the blanket again. "But you know, I've eaten the finest Belgian and Swiss chocolates in the world since I've grown up, and I don't believe any of it has ever tasted any better to me than that awful junk we ate as kids.''

"The point is, do you still eat gumdrops and caramel suckers?''

Sadie shook her head. ''Not on a bet. A kid's delight is an adult's abomination.''

Reese's eyes narrowed to slits. ''Maybe there's hope your taste in other things will develop with maturity,'' he said softly. After a brief, tense silence, he handed her a stick that he'd sharpened at the tip. ''Fire's ready,'' he said. ''Shall we dine?''

They set to the serious business of roasting a hot dog to its natural perfection, juicy and sizzling on the inside, crusty and brown on the outside. They finished almost simultaneously and buried the hot dogs in soft buns slathered with mustard and sprinkled with chopped onion.

"Delicious!'' Sadie pronounced.

"How about some cold pork and beans?'' Reese flipped open the top and handed her a one-portion can and a plastic spoon.

"An epicure's delight.'' Sadie munched on her hot dog, then reached for the bag of chips.

"If only I had a cold beer, it would be perfect.'' Reese stretched out on his side and gave all his attention to his food. They ate in a companionable silence that dissipated their earlier anger. ''Too bad we don't have a radio so we could listen to some music,'' Reese said.

"We have the birds," Sadie said. "There isn't any music more beautiful than theirs."

"It's a little hard to dance to, though."

Sadie giggled. "Maybe we could line up the birds on that tree branch and teach them how to keep time to a metronome."

Reese waved his arm, conducting an imaginary orchestra of birds. "Now for the robins," he said. "That's it—two, three, four—join in, cardinals, one, two—mockingbirds, your turn—"

"No blue jays or starlings," insisted Sadie. "They make noise, not music."

"Ah, but would other blue jays and starlings agree?"

Sadie tossed a chip at him. "Oh, Reese, how like you to take the side of a squawking old blue jay."

"That's because I know how it feels to be a blue jay when you want to be a bright cardinal everybody loves."

"Everybody always loved you, Reese. Everybody."

He shook his head. "Everybody *respected* me. It was Jerry Don they *loved*."

"That isn't true." Sadie shook her head. "We all loved you. We still do."

Their glances met and held. "Why do you say it that way?" Reese asked. "Why first person *plural*?"

"What's wrong with saying *we* love you? That means more people, and more love." Sadie felt a sudden need to retreat. What would it mean to say '*I* love you' to Reese? She loved him, of course—she always had—but saying it *that* way meant something different, something threatening—and probably something untrue. They weren't ready to test the character of her love. It would spoil their day. "Besides," Sadie said, changing the subject, "what's wrong with being respected? I should think most people would prefer that."

"Do you respect me, Sadie?"

"Of course."

"Can you bring yourself to say it?" He was taunting her now for being unable to say she loved him.

"Yes, Reese, I respect you. I always have, and I always will. I respect you more than anyone I've ever known. I respect you the way the soldiers at Valley Forge respected George Washington. I respect you the way the ancient Egyptians respected the Pharaoh. I respect you the way—"

He let her lay the flattery on so thickly that she finally started giggling at her own inventiveness. "Thank you, Sadie," he said solemnly. "Does that mean that you'll still respect me if I make love with you?"

She burst into surprised laughter. "It was a trap!" she said, gasping for breath.

"And you fell for it."

"I forgot how clever you are."

"You haven't answered my question." He was moving toward her on the blanket.

"We haven't toasted our marshmallows."

"I'm not hungry right now."

"I'm all sweaty," she protested.

"So am I."

"Then we should wait."

"This is our last day."

She'd run out of excuses. "I'm scared, Reese."

"Why?"

"I'm afraid I'll never be the same afterward."

"So am I."

"You're scared, too?" She'd never known Reese to be afraid of anything.

"But I'm more afraid of not finding out."

"Finding out what?"

"What it's like to make love to you."

She lowered her lashes. There was so much intensity in Reese she could sense it in his pores, see it in his eyes. "Reese, what if Jerry Don's ghost won't stay buried while we're making love?"

"Jerry Don's ghost is never going to stay buried until you quit coaxing it out of his grave with all those promises and sweet talk." Reese reached to touch Sadie for the first time, and she could tell that he was fighting back his anger in order to help her. "No one can do that but you, Sadie. *I* said goodbye to Jerry Don a long time ago. *You*'re the one that won't let go."

Her eyes filled with tears. "I don't know how," she whispered.

Reese stood and pulled Sadie up with him, then firmly steered her toward the creek bank. When they reached the sand, he gently pushed her down and squatted beside her. "Dig," he said. "Dig a hole and put Jerry Don's ghost in it. While you're at it, bury all that guilt you're carrying around with you. Dig until your arms are tired, and when the hole is finally big enough to hold all that garbage from the past, bury it, Sadie. Pack it down with sand so it can't get out and haunt you anymore."

"Will you help me?" she whimpered. Tears were falling down her cheeks now. The whole thing sounded crazy to her, yet there was something so compelling about it that she was already digging in the sand with her hands.

"Nobody can do this but you, Sadie. It's your own private grief. I'll be at the camp fire. When you're ready, I'll be waiting for you."

He left her with the warm sun beating on her back, the sand moist and crumbling beneath her fingers. She hollowed out a hole, but as she thought of Jerry Don and the radiance of first love, she knew she needed a bigger grave to hold it. Tears dripped down her cheeks and fell into the sand, and she was filled with an overpowering sadness for a love that had been cut short. In some strange way, that love passed before her eyes in all its youthful glory, then flowed through her fingers into the earth, to be followed by memories of the hateful times at the end when she and Jerry Don had argued and bickered. Her tears became sobs, but her guilt lessened as she let go of it and forced it into an earthly grave. Her emotions spilled over, and she was surprised to discover that she'd been suppressing a terrible anger toward Jerry Don for all these years.

"You left me with nothing, Jerry Don," she cried, pounding the earth. "All those plans we made, and they all died with you. You knew how much I wanted to have children with you, and you stole that dream from me. You took my heart with you and left me with nothing! Inside I've been a bitter, shriveled-up old woman hiding behind a cheerleader's smile, and all because of you."

The words had poured from Sadie's lips with such abandon she hardly knew what she was saying. It was only the thought of Reese that brought her up short and drove the hysteria from her mind. She sank silently beside the hole she'd dug and stared into it.

She took a handful of sand and sprinkled it into the hole. "In memory of Jerry Don Wallace, who died too soon," she said. "May we all find peace at last." Her emotions were spent. Buried in the hole were her anger, her guilt, her self-pity. For the first time in six years, she felt free. She scooped the piled-up sand back into the hole and pounded until it was level again. By the time the sun had beaten on it for an hour, no one would ever know the earth had been disturbed. Nature would heal its wound.

She stood and said a silent prayer over the place where she'd buried her past. Then she walked toward the creek. She wanted to wash away her tears before she went to join Reese.

Chapter Nine

Sadie walked along the creek bed until she found a place at the edge of a sandstone bluff where there was a pool of water deep enough for bathing. It was high noon, and there was no escape from the penetrating sunlight.

She stripped off her jeans and thin, long-sleeved shirt and tossed them beside the cowboy hat she'd borrowed from Dwaine Pickens and the cowboy boots she'd had since high school. Next she peeled off her underwear, rinsed it in the clear creek water, then spread it on a juniper bush to dry. As lightly as a sea nymph, she eased herself into the cool water.

The water was only waist high, and she bent to splash her face and dunk her head, delighting as cool rivulets washed through her hair and trickled down her neck and shoulders. There was scarcely room enough to swim in the pool, but Sadie made the effort to submerge herself and take a few breaststrokes. Her whole body felt clean and alive, and she propelled herself to the surface with a loud whoop of pleasure before diving underwater again. Below her, variegated pink-and-white sandstone pebbles kept the water crystal clear, and the constant movement of the creek prevented moss from forming and clouding the pool.

Sadie wondered whether anyone had ever swum in this creek, remote as it was from the rest of humanity. Maybe only a few Plains Indians or some prehistoric nomads, she decided, and no one had left a trace except the busy prairie dogs that had built their dam there. It was both humbling and exhilarating to realize she'd found a secret primeval treasure. She coiled herself and thrust upward to the surface again, shaking the wet hair back from her face and preening at her reflection in the water. She looked like a young girl again, joyful and enthusiastic. Laughing aloud from the sheer pleasure of being alive, she dived again.

A hand reached out and pulled her close. She turned. Somehow Reese had worked his way across and down the edge of the cliff, then slipped into the water without her noticing. His body was wet and cool and naked next to her own, his arms strong around her waist. Sadie's hair streamed outward from her shoulders in the water as she moved into his embrace. As one, they floated upward to the surface, mouth clinging to mouth, bodies intertwined.

"Sadie, Sadie," Reese whispered, as though he couldn't have enough of saying her name. "My precious Sadie. I've waited so long for this moment." He stroked her soft, satiny flesh, moving from waist to breast to hip as he murmured incoherently about her beauty and his desire.

Sadie reached for palmfuls of cool water and trickled it across Reese's shoulders and back, then traced his dark eyebrows and lashes with the remaining droplets. His cheeks were warm between her hands, and she outlined his features with her fingers, moving from the smooth skin on his cheekbones to the rough stubble at his chin. All nature was hushed as she and Reese embraced, and the only sounds were the ripple of the water in the pool and the roaring of passion in their ears.

"This place is like the beginning of creation," Sadie whispered. "We can almost believe we're the only people in the world."

Reese smiled. "I think I know how Adam felt when he woke up and discovered Eve lying beside him."

Sadie tilted her head, considering the proposition. "And how did Adam feel?" she asked.

"Procreative."

They laughed in unison.

"And how did Eve feel on that fateful morning?" Reese asked with a curious lift of one eyebrow.

Sadie drew back enough so that she could view his entire body. Her cheeks brightened, and there was a huskiness in her voice when she answered. "Eve was absolutely amazed."

Their glances met and locked. Sadie felt her heart begin to pound with a crazy, erratic rhythm. Then Reese scooped her into his arms, pressing her body close against his. "Kiss me, Sadie," he demanded in a voice roughened with desire as he sought her lips. His tongue probed her mouth, teasing a fiery response from her that surprised both of them. She clasped her hands at the base of his neck, pulling his head downward into a more forceful plunder of her mouth. Fully impassioned, she nipped his bottom lip, then smiled when he moaned with pleasure.

She leaned back in his arms, breaking the kiss so his mouth could move down her neck, nuzzle her throat, then fasten upon her breast with moist, desperate urgings. His lower body pushed against her thighs, demanding entry. Caught in a maelstrom of pleasure, she responded with total abandon. In that moment she would have given him anything, done anything he asked. Almost shyly, she took his hand and led him from the pool, then lowered herself onto the warm sand and opened her arms to him.

"Sadie—" he said, choked with emotion as he cradled her body with his. "So long I've wanted— dreamed—" His mouth searched for hers, and their kiss turned to liquid fire, setting him ablaze and the world with it.

Sadie teased him again with her teeth and heard the same gasp of pleasure the gesture had evoked before. Emboldened by her power over him, she searched for his earlobe and gave it a nip, then gently licked until he broke away.

"No more," he murmured. "It's more pleasure than I can handle." He was too aroused for tenderness, too close to the edge to go slowly or hold back.

"It's okay, Reese. Nothing is going to stop us this time," she said, her eyes half closed and sensual. She found his other earlobe and gave him a sharp bite.

"Sadie, sweetheart, don't. I don't want to rush you." The look on his face was almost one of pain from his trying to quench a passion that was burning out of control.

In response, Sadie brought Reese's hand to her breast, then let her own hand roam down to his waist and across his hips. As she stroked, she saw that his face had taken on an expression of exquisite pleasure. Overwhelmed by the urgency of his desire, and her own need to fulfill it, she shifted underneath him and eased his entry inside her.

He thrust with long, hard strokes, filling her while he murmured her name and moaned aloud. With his hands and mouth he sought to pleasure her even as she did him. Locked in a primitive embrace, they gave freely all they had to give, becoming part of all nature in their physical mating.

Afterwards, Reese pulled Sadie into a loose embrace, gently stroking her long, damp locks of hair.

Their sudden, overpowering physical intimacy had left them with no need for words. Reese had many questions, but for now he kept them to himself. Besides, their lovemaking had left them sleepy and lethargic. Sadie snuggled in his arms as though she were content to stay there forever.

They dozed until the sun grew uncomfortably hot on their bare skin and wakened them.

Sadie sat up and yawned, stretching her arms high over her head. "I think my back must be sunburned," she said, trying to see over her shoulder.

Reese lay on his back and smiled up at her. "Your nose has a few freckles."

"Reese Chandler, you aren't looking at my nose."

He lifted himself on one elbow and scooped her breast into his hand. He flicked the nipple with his tongue until it responded. "You have a cute nose," he said, chuckling, "but it doesn't have the fascination that this part of you has."

"Fascination? Why?"

"Because you can't control the way it responds to me. When it likes what I do, it lets me know."

Sadie pushed Reese onto the sand and eased her body above his. "Every part of my body likes everything you do to it. I can't control any of my reactions when you're making love to me." She gave him a complacent smile. "I surrendered myself to you completely, Reese. Couldn't you tell?"

A lump formed in Reese's throat, making it hard for him to swallow. "Oh, yes, I could tell."

Overcome with tenderness for Sadie, Reese felt his eyes moisten with unshed tears. She'd given herself to him physically, but emotionally she was still holding something back. He must have her heart as well as her body, and time was running out on him.

He caressed her, watching as she relaxed and sighed with pleasure. The physical passion he aroused in her was her only vulnerability where Reese was concerned. The one thing he must not do was rush her or pressure her—not now, not when she was enduring the pain of facing the past and relinquishing it. Only when she'd made her peace with her adolescent love for Jerry Don would she be ready for a mature, whole relationship.

"Sadie," he said gently, holding her close against his chest. "Why didn't you tell me this was the first time for you?"

She shrugged, as though embarrassed by the question. "I did, sort of. I kept saying there was nobody else for me after Jerry Don died. It was like we'd really gotten married, almost, and I had to be faithful to his memory."

Reese clenched his jaw, but otherwise he controlled his reaction. "Were you going to waste your whole life as some kind of vestal virgin keeping a holy shrine?"

"Call me old-fashioned," she said, smiling as she traced a fingernail across his bare chest. "But I couldn't go to bed with some guy I didn't care about. With you it's different. I feel safe even when you're stirring up the most thrilling sensations in me."

"Are you going to regret this tomorrow?"

"Of course not. It was the most wonderful experience of my life." Her dazzling smile was proof of her sincerity. "What about you, Reese? Will you regret it tomorrow?"

For an answer he kissed her fully on the mouth. When they finally broke apart, he said, "The only thing I regret is that I have to take you home now. Your mother was expecting us an hour ago."

There was a glint of mischief in Sadie's eyes. "If we're already late, what's another half hour?"

Reese tangled his hands in her hair and pulled her face to his. Sadie's breathing quickened as his hands began their sure, knowing strokes.

"One question," she said, "while I can still talk. What do you have in mind for an encore?"

"I'm back, Mom," Sadie called as she tried to slip into her bedroom without stopping to talk. "Are you doing okay?"

"Fine, dear. Did you have a good day?"

Sadie gave a noncommittal response. She really didn't want to join her mother and Al Peterson in the living room right now. Instead, she wanted to retreat into the privacy of her own room and bask in memories of the day spent with Reese. Never had Sadie felt so alive and radiant, and she wanted to prolong the wonderful afterglow of lovemaking.

"Come join us for a glass of iced tea, dear," Nelda insisted. "It's so hot today."

"In a few minutes, Mom. I'm all sweaty from riding horseback. I need to take a quick shower." With that, Sadie firmly shut her bedroom door. At least she could repair her disheveled hair and clothes before she had to endure her mother's scrutiny.

She went into the connecting bathroom and adjusted the water to a pleasant, cool spray. Each place the needles of water touched her body was a place where Reese's hands and lips had touched, caressed, lingered. Sadie leaned her head back and let the water cascade over her, remembering the way her body and Reese's had intertwined in the pool only a short time before.

With a start, Sadie realized that she was humming. It was the same song Reese had whistled early that morning: "Ladies love outlaws..." Sadie smiled and turned off the water. Nobody would ever consider Reese an "outlaw." He was too disciplined, too much a straight arrow for that. And yet the passion of his lovemaking had shattered all restraints and inhibitions between them.

Sadie wrapped her wet hair in a towel and wondered whether she would ever be the same again. It was as though she and Reese had truly become one person in that joyous consummation of male and female flesh. How could she go into the living room and carry on a normal conversation when she was so full of awe?

"More iced tea, anybody?" she asked, getting a frosty pitcher from the kitchen before she joined her mother and Al Peterson in the living room. As she poured refills, she felt her mother's thoughtful glance following her.

"Sadie, Al has been telling me about a new program the high school will offer next year. He's applied for a grant to help the children of migrant farm workers."

Al Peterson was a big, raw-boned man, ruddy-faced and white-haired, with a voice which always surprised his listeners because it was so gentle and soft-spoken. He appeared to be the kind of man whose voice would boom to the top of the gymnasium, yet he had maintained order and decorum during his twenty years as principal of Tascosa High School by speaking in a slow, quiet drawl. "We've been approved for the grant," he said, "but if we don't hire a new principal right away, there's not going to be time to get the program started."

"And the school will forfeit the grant." Nelda sounded dismayed at the prospect. "School is so hard for migrant children. It will be a real shame if the program falls through."

Sadie was drawn into the conversation despite suspicions that her mother was taking advantage of the local problem. Sadie had a natural sympathy for migrant children, who had such tremendous odds to overcome in order to get any kind of education at all. She was impressed that an almost retired, small-town principal like Al Peterson would have gone through the bureaucratic maze and unending paperwork to get a federal grant approved.

"Hoped to get something started that someone else could build on," Al said, shrugging off Sadie's compliments. "Isn't that what teaching is all about—building for the future?" He gathered up the papers he'd been working on and stuffed them into a folder. "Maybe the school board will decide on a new principal pretty soon. I sure hope someone will be on the job next month, or this migrant grant is a lost cause."

"Reese says you've received ten applications for the principal's job," Sadie responded. "Do any of them look like good candidates?"

"Fair, fair. The best one has his eye set on being a superintendent in a couple of years, so he wouldn't be with us for long. We may have to settle for him, though. The school board wants to wait a little longer in hopes of getting someone for the long haul, but they know they'll have to make a decision soon. There's not much point in worrying about who's going to be around in the future if there's nobody in the job right now."

"I've been trying to get Sadie to apply for the job. She's got her administrator's certification from the University of Texas, you know." Nelda made her statement as though it were a brand-new idea, but Sadie suspected it had been the topic of the day's conversation between her mother and the principal. She became convinced she was right when Al cleared his throat and flushed a little before responding.

"Well, now, that sounds like a mighty fine idea," he said. "I know the school board would love to have your application, Sadie. I'll drop one off for you if you think you're interested. Or let me see—I might have one with me in all these papers." He thumbed through his folder and withdrew a blank application. "Sure enough," he said, "here's one."

He handed it to Sadie, and she couldn't be rude to him by refusing it. It wasn't his fault that her mother had put him in such an untenable position. "Thank you, Mr. Peterson," she said, placing the application on the coffee table in front of her.

"Call me *Al*, why don't you? And let me know if I can help you make up your mind. You can come over to the high school, and I'll go over all the plans and schedules with you. We've got a good program, Sadie. You could be real proud of being a principal at Tascosa. And Tascosa would be real lucky to have you."

"Thank you. I'll think about it and let you know." Sadie gathered up the empty tea glasses and carried them into the kitchen. She was quite put out with her mother for having trapped her in an awkward situation. When she returned to the living room, her mother was seeing Al to the door.

"Thank you for coming by," Nelda said, giving him a warm smile. "I certainly enjoyed our visit. When I get off these crutches and can get around better, maybe you can come for supper some evening."

"That would be real nice. It's been mighty lonely for me the past few months since my wife passed on." He stretched out his hand and gave her a hearty handshake, then turned to Sadie. "You take care to have a safe trip back to Austin tomorrow. I hope you'll decide you've had enough of the city and beat a trail straight back to Tascosa." He put on his straw hat, then doffed it at least twice before he backed out the door. "See you soon, Nelda. And let me know if I can do any errands for you after Sadie's gone." He waved several times, then got into his pickup truck and tooted the horn goodbye.

The women returned to the living room, and Sadie found herself laughing as the truck disappeared down the dirt road, its horn tooting again at the crossroads.

"What's so funny?" Nelda was not amused.

"Mr. Peterson," Sadie said, laughing again. "He's smitten with you, Mom. If Jerry Don had honked his horn at me for a mile down the road, you'd have boiled him in oil. And here *you* are with a sixty-five-year-old gentleman caller who's probably going to run into a fence post because he's looking back at you while he's driving his pickup."

"I'll thank you not to ridicule our guest. He went out of his way to be kind to me today so *you* could gallivant around the county with Reese. I had no idea you'd be gone so long, or I wouldn't have imposed on Mr. Peterson that way."

"*Mr.* Peterson? He said to call him Al." Sadie dissolved into laughter again. "I'm sorry, Mom, but you have to admit this is a strange turn of events. I went off with Reese, and it turns out *you* were the one who needed a chaperon!''

Nelda gave her daughter a jaundiced glance. "Don't forget that I caught a glimpse of you when you returned home, Sadie. I have a notion that you were in greater need of a chaperon than I was."

Sadie's smile remained exactly as it was. *"Me?"* she asked innocently. "You raised me to be an old-fashioned girl, Mom, and that's exactly what I've been." It was probably a lie, she thought, but only of degree. Until two hours previously, the statement had been perfectly true. And what happened two hours ago was none of her mother's business.

Nelda sighed. "I really don't want to argue with you on your last day, Sadie." She arranged her leg with its plaster cast on a footstool and leaned back in an overstuffed chair.

Sadie kicked off her sandals and settled into the corner of the sofa, her feet drawn up beneath her. "I don't want to argue, either."

"I raised you to be a decent girl," Nelda continued, "but I certainly didn't expect you to bury yourself alive when Jerry Don died. You're young, and you need to find someone to love. Reese seems to be a perfect choice, and if I were a young woman, I'd go after him with everything in my power. But if you won't have Reese, find someone else before it's too late."

"Too late for what?"

"Too late to have a family." Nelda gave her daughter an earnest glance. "And too late to *love*, Sadie. When you shut yourself off, you forget how to love. That's what I did when your father died. I wrapped myself into a cocoon and pretended my world had shrunk that small. It's been safe for me there, but, oh, my, it's been so confining and so lonely in that cocoon, Sadie. I didn't realize until today how much I want to break free from it. I think I've been a bad example for you."

Her mother's revelation surprised Sadie. How could anybody make such a complete turnaround in one morning? Why hadn't her mother had to struggle as Sadie had to work through her grief and isolation?

"What happened this morning, Mom?" she asked.

"Nothing, really. I just found that I enjoyed drinking a morning cup of coffee with a man again, that's all."

"And just like that," Sadie said, snapping her fingers, "you figured out what was wrong? It seems too simple."

"Oh, I think it's been in the back of my mind for a long time, but I just wouldn't face up to it—until I broke my leg and had to stay in bed, with nothing to do but think. Sometimes the good Lord takes advantage of our troubles to help us mend our ways."

"But how can you know in one morning that you want to marry Al Peterson?"

"Whatever makes you think that's what I want to do?" Suddenly Nelda was defensive.

"Mom, it was written all over your face—and his, too. I suppose you've been acquainted with each other for years, but you don't really *know* each other. And I don't exactly think it was a case of love at first sight. You can't possibly be in love with him—are you?"

"No, no, of course not." Nelda lifted her hands, entreating understanding. "But when you get old, Sadie, you know you don't have time to waste. Al and I haven't said a word to each other about this yet, but I suppose we both recognize that we're compatible, we're lonely, we have the same values, and we have something to offer each other. At this stage of life, that's a pretty good bargain. If we insisted on romantic love, too, we'd end our days alone. That kind of love is the luxury and self-indulgence of the young."

"Mom, you sound so cynical! I remember how you felt about Daddy, and all the stories you told me about your courtship. You treasured those romantic memories, so please don't pretend now that it wasn't important to you!"

"Maybe it's easier to compromise now and settle for what I *can* have instead of what I'd *like* to have. Or maybe I've gotten more bitter in my cocoon than I realized," Nelda admitted.

"Tell me the truth, Mom. Would you want me to marry someone I didn't love with all my heart?"

"Ah, but Sadie, you never love someone with all your heart *before* you get married. That comes later, child, after you've made sacrifices for him and cared for him when he's sick and discouraged and helped him build a life and a family—when what happens to *him* is more important than what happens to *you* and there's no selfishness at all in your love, because you want to *give* instead of *take*."

"That's a pretty tall order, Mom. I think it would take a saint to fill it."

"And what do you think a saint is, Sadie? Isn't it just an ordinary person doing ordinary things, but doing them for the benefit of someone else?"

"Give me an example."

"Well, dear, like the baby rabbit Reese brought you. Reese went to a lot of trouble because he knows you love helpless creatures. He thought the rabbit would be a comfort to you and maybe you wouldn't be so unhappy."

"Did he tell you that?"

"Of course not. But I've known Reese a long time, and we've grown close during the years since your father died and he's run the farm for me. He doesn't say much, but he's always doing little acts of kindness."

Sadie felt a wrenching pain in her heart. "Mom, he asked me what I was going to do with the rabbit when I left, and I told him I'd give it to Wynona's children. I didn't realize what it meant to him. I must have hurt his feelings something awful."

"I'm sure he understands that you can't keep a rabbit in your tiny apartment. If it made you happy for even a few hours, he'll be glad he gave it to you."

Sadie got up and paced the room. How could she have been so callous? She loved Sniffles, and she hadn't meant to reject Reese's gift. What could she do to make amends?

"Tell me what to do, Mom. I've got to do something to make things right with Reese. I've hurt him enough over the years without hurting him again as my final act on my way out of town."

"Sadie, forgive me, but haven't you lost sight of our conversation? It isn't the *rabbit* that's important, dear. What's important is that Reese loves you and brought you the rabbit as an expression of his love. You're getting the two things confused."

"Mom, Reese doesn't love me, not the way we were talking about." Sadie couldn't entertain that possibility. Even to herself, she couldn't deny the overwhelming sexual attraction she and Reese felt for each other. But passion wasn't love, and by itself it wasn't very romantic.

"I think you're wrong, Sadie. I think Reese has always loved you. Just as you've always loved him."

"For heaven's sake, Mom, romantic love isn't the same thing as the love of friendship." Sadie felt herself growing defensive. Her mother was pushing her into a corner, and she wasn't sure herself what she felt for Reese. Excitement, yes. Love, no. As far as her mother was concerned, she wasn't ready to admit to anything but friendship. "Reese and I are friends, we like each other, we have things in common, just as you and Mr. Peterson do. That's all. I asked you if you'd want me to marry someone if I didn't love him with my whole heart. I *want* romantic love, Mom. That's not what I feel for Reese, and that's not what he feels for me. We have a perfectly wonderful friendship, but that's all it is. I'm not going to settle for that, not yet. If I do, I'll cheat myself out of the real thing. If that's enough for you, that's fine. Maybe when I reach your age, I'll feel the same way. But I'm only twenty-eight years old, Mom! There's got to be something more for me." She was on the verge of tears.

"Sadie, please, dear, don't upset yourself anymore. You don't have to decide anything today. You take your time, and when your thoughts are clear, you'll know what to do. I won't pressure you anymore about coming back to Tascosa. It was wrong of me, even though I thought it was in your best interest. I'm sorry, dear, to have made you unhappy."

Nelda held out her arms, and Sadie went to kneel beside her mother's chair to take comfort in her arms. She took a deep breath and repeated the question that was nagging at her mind.

"Mom, what on earth am I going to do about Sniffles? Reese is coming to pick me up at seven o'clock to have supper with Tom and Wynona. I've got to have an answer before he gets here."

Nelda gently stroked Sadie's hair. "You'll think of something, dear. Just follow your heart, and do what it tells you."

Sadie kept her gaze averted as the color rose in her cheeks. Where Reese Chandler was concerned, it wasn't her heart that caused the problem. It was the way her body responded to his.

Chapter Ten

As seven o'clock drew near, Sadie found herself with a fluttering pulse and butterflies in her stomach. She could hardly wait for Reese to arrive and rekindle the physical sensations he'd aroused in her that afternoon. She almost wished they didn't have to go to the Evanses' for dinner so they could have the time alone for more lovemaking.

Sadie was stunned by the depth of her response to Reese. All these years she'd cloistered herself sexually, and it was as though the fires of her passion, once ignited, could not be extinguished. The mere memory of his kisses, his hands, his body, brought color to her cheeks and desire to the very core of her being. She bathed, then powdered and perfumed herself with extra care.

She tried on and rejected every garment she'd brought from Austin. She'd already worn the green gauze outfit several times, and otherwise she'd brought only shorts, T-shirts, and sports clothes. Finally she checked the closet to see if there was anything left over from her school days and found a scoop-neck pink-and-white gingham dress with tiny puff sleeves that she'd worn to a summer sorority party at college. She held her breath while she buttoned the dress, hopeful it would still fit her. It had been snug in the waist six years ago, but her waist was slimmer now, and instead it was the bodice that was too tight over her breasts.

She turned first one way and then the other, considering the problem she saw reflected in the mirror. Then, on an impulse, she searched for an eyelet-lace ruffled camisole and petticoat she remembered seeing somewhere. She found them in a sacheted drawer, the crisp white fabric permeated with the bouquet of wild roses. She removed the dress, put on the lacy undergarments, and when she slipped back into the dress, she left open two buttons at the neck where the dress was too tight, and four buttons at the hem.

She gave her mirrored reflection a triumphant smile. The dress was perfect—feminine and coy in an old-fashioned way, yet also flirtatious and sexy. Reese Chandler was going to have a hard time keeping his eyes off her tonight.

Humming to herself, Sadie brushed her hair, grateful that it had as much gold as red in its pigment so that she could wear pink. She'd just fastened dangling gold earrings at her lobes when the doorbell rang. Her heart immediately began to race, but before she left her room, she made a final adjustment to her neckline, tugging the camisole a little lower.

"Sadie, Reese is here," her mother called from the living room, where she was watching TV.

Sadie added a last dab of rosy-pink lip gloss. Now she was ready. "I'll be right out."

Reese was standing on the front porch, ready to ring the doorbell again, when Sadie opened the door. He looked so splendid in navy dress slacks and a light blue loose-knit cotton sweater that Sadie could only swallow hard and choke out, "I didn't realize you were so handsome."

"Flattery will get you everywhere with me," he said, flushing a little at Sadie's frank admiration. As they lingered in the secluded entryway, he, too, swallowed hard. "You're so beautiful you take my breath away." He took her hand, lifted it to his lips and kissed her inner palm, then her wrist. She put her other arm around his shoulder to draw him nearer to her, and he bent to brush her mouth with a gentle kiss.

When she and Reese drew apart, her lashes were glistening with tears.

"What's wrong, sweetheart?"

At a loss for words, she could only shrug. How could she express the tenderness and sweetness she'd experienced in their kiss?

Reese cupped her chin between his two strong hands and kissed the tip of her nose. Smiling into her eyes, he asked, "What have you been doing all afternoon?"

Sadie decided to tease him with an honest answer. "Thinking about what we did at noon and counting the minutes until tonight."

Reese blushed again. "I didn't know you had such greedy appetites."

Sadie leaned in his arms so that in order to hold her upright, Reese had to draw her lower torso against his. "There are a lot of things about me that you don't know, Mr. Chandler. I think you're in for a few surprises."

He chuckled, saying, "I can't help wondering if you aren't surprising yourself as much as you are me, Sadie."

Now it was Sadie's turn to blush. "Wonder all you please," she said. "But I'll never tell." She slid her arms around his neck and drank in the light, musky scent of his after-shave. "Now give me one real kiss," she insisted, "and then we need to go. Wynona will be wondering what happened to her dinner guests."

Several kisses later, when their breathing had become ragged and Sadie's mouth felt sweetly bruised, she and Reese reluctantly drew apart.

"Those green eyes of yours look sultry," Reese observed.

"Hazel."

"Not tonight. Green with golden fires. Sexiest eyes I've ever seen."

"Will anybody notice?" Sadie asked.

"Does it matter?"

"Well, of course. I don't want people speculating about us. It's nobody's business what we do."

"This is a small town. People are curious, and naturally they're going to wonder what's going on between us. This is probably the most exciting thing to happen in Tascosa in ages, now that they've got two single people of the opposite sex to gossip about."

"How do you stand it, Reese, knowing that people are watching every move you make?"

He laughed. "I make sure that certain moves don't transpire in Tascosa where people can see."

"So that's why you do your socializing in other towns!" Suddenly Sadie was as curious as any town gossip buzzing over the back fence. "How many girl-friends do you have, anyway?"

"Dozens. I find there's safety in numbers."

Sadie couldn't help herself. She was jealous. "Do you take them to the ranch and roast hot dogs and splash naked in the pool with them, too?"

"No," he answered seriously, drawing her face close and brushing her eyelids with feathery kisses. "Never. No one but you."

"You promise?"

He held up his right hand, palm out. "Scout's honor, hope to die."

She brightened and gave him a relieved smile. "We had such a wonderful day, didn't we? I'll never forget it as long as I live."

Reese scooped her into his arms and held her tightly. "It's about time you had some happy memories to go with the sad ones."

"Will it be a happy memory for you, too?" Sadie asked, then felt suddenly shy at what his answer might be.

He struggled for words to express himself. "It was every dream I ever had, come true. It was the best, Sadie. When I'm an old man, that memory will warm my cold, dark days." His head came down, and gently, ever so gently, he brushed her lips with his.

"We have to go, Reese," Sadie said at last. "Because if we don't go now, I'm going to take you in my bedroom and shut the door and make love to you until the sun comes up."

Reese let go of Sadie and stepped apart from her. "Let me get this straight. Choice A: have supper with Tom and Wynona. Choice B: make love with you all night." He snapped his fingers. "Nothing to it. Choice A, of course. I'm starving. Aren't you?"

Sadie reached for his hand. "Let's tell Mom goodnight. She'll probably go to bed early, since she didn't have a nap this afternoon." Sadie giggled. "You know what, Reese? I think Mom and Mr. Peterson are going to get married. Isn't that a surprise?"

"Not to me."

"You already suspected?"

"Just call me Cupid."

They walked into the living room hand in hand and found Nelda dozing in her chair, the TV program forgotten.

"I'd better help her get to bed," Sadie whispered. "She's exhausted, poor thing. I believe she's had too much excitement for one day."

"While you get her to bed, I'll load the rabbit hutch in the back of my truck. The kids will jump for joy when we walk in with Sniffles."

Sadie reached out her hand to stop him from leaving. "No, Reese. I changed my mind."

"What do you mean? You can't leave the rabbit here for your mom to take care of, Sadie. She can't make it to the garden on those crutches to pick vegetables for it to eat. Or do you plan to play Cupid, too, and give Al Peterson an excuse to come by every day?"

"No, I hadn't thought of that. That's not what I want to do, though. Mom doesn't care anything about rabbits. Sniffles would feel rejected if I left him here. I'm going to take him back to Austin with me in the morning."

"Sadie, that's nuts. You can't keep a rabbit in an apartment."

"Yes, I can. I have a little patio, and I'll put a cage out there for him. He'll do just fine."

"What's gotten into you?" Reese asked, puzzled at Sadie's unexpected behavior. "At least leave him with Wynona's kids. They'll keep him company and play with him."

Sadie shook her head. "They'll roughhouse with him, you mean. Sniffles is little and helpless, and he needs *me*, Reese. I'm the one who loves him and feeds him every day. Besides, he'll keep me from getting so lonesome. I need Sniffles as much as he needs me. And you know that, Reese. That's why you brought him to me."

"Well, sure, but . . ."

"But what?"

"But you're happier now. You don't need him the way you did last week."

"In some ways I need him even more," Sadie said quietly. "I need him to remind me of my oldest and best friend, who cared that I was hurting and tried to ease my pain."

Reese dropped a kiss on the top of Sadie's head. "You're sure?" he asked, still questioning her decision.

She nodded assent and was rewarded with the most radiant smile she'd ever seen. Tears sprang to her eyes, and she quickly shook them away. "Let's get Mom to bed," she said. "If we're lucky, she'll still be sleeping this soundly when you bring me home tonight."

* * *

Tom Evans greeted them at the door with a hearty handshake, and Wynona hurried from the kitchen, the baby propped on one hip.

"Thank goodness you were late, hon. Melanie picked tonight to be fussy, and I'm still trying to finish putting things together for supper."

"I'm hungry, Mommy," yelled Biff, then fell to the floor with a loud scream. "I'm dead. Aaron killed me."

Aaron ran through the room, his toy cowboy gun clicking madly. "Take that, and that, you bank robber!"

Becka came stumbling into the living room, a handkerchief tied across her eyes. "I'm the hostage," she lisped. "Won't someone please save me?"

Tom Evans sat down in his recliner, oblivious to the kids' commotion, and offered Sadie and Reese the sofa. "How long before supper?" he asked Wynona.

"Sometime before midnight, I hope." She handed the baby to Tom. "See if you can keep her quiet for a little while, won't you?"

Tom straddled the baby on one leg and made faces at her. "What's wrong with Daddy's baby girl?" he asked. "Did you miss your favorite television program?"

The baby let out a yell.

"Oh-oh. What's wrong with her, Wynona?"

"Nothing. She's spoiled, that's all." Wynona, who was usually so patient, seemed to be at her wit's end.

"Will you children *please* try to act civilized while we have company?" she pleaded. "Do you guys want a beer while we finish up supper?"

"Sounds good to me," said Tom.

"Can I have a swig, Daddy?" asked Biff.

"I'll take a swig of Reese's," Aaron said.

"I don't like beer, because I'm a girl," Becka said. "Will somebody please rescue me so I can see again?"

Sadie bent down to untie the handkerchief that bound Becka's eyes.

Aaron immediately stuck his cowboy pistol in Sadie's back and fired. "You're dead, Sadie! Fall on the floor!"

Sadie went down on all fours.

Aaron let out a loud guffaw of laughter. "I got you, I got you!" He moved closer, but Sadie kept her eyes closed and played dead. When he bent over to see whether she was breathing, she lunged for him and dragged him onto the floor, tickling him under his arms and on his sides. He kicked and squirmed and laughed like a hyena, enjoying the attention. The twins demanded their turns at being tickled, too, then giggled until they were pink-faced and out of breath.

Aaron made a face, twisting his lips inside out and making his eyes cross by focusing on his nose. "Bet you can't make a face like that," he said.

Sadie smiled at him. "No, and I don't even want to try. It's too ugly. What if it got stuck and I had to spend the rest of my life that way?"

He gave a disgusted snort. "It won't get stuck," he insisted. For proof, he made another face even worse than the first. "Are you a sissy or something?"

There was something familiar about his taunt, and Sadie studied him and tried to recall what it was. There was an elusive memory, just beyond reach. Maybe she would remember later on. "How many people are hungry?" she asked. "Raise your hands so I can count."

Hands went up around the room. "Hold up your hand, Reese," said Becka, crawling onto his lap while she kept her chubby fingers held high. "Daddy, hold up Melanie's hand." She snuggled against Reese's chin. "Mmm, you smell nice," she said, and gave him a big kiss on the cheek.

"You better watch out, Sadie," Wynona said in a droll voice. "A younger woman is beating your time."

Rising from her place on the floor, Sadie caught Reese's eye. "It's that after-shave of yours," she said. "It knocks them dead every time."

Grinning, he answered, "I guess I better start buying it by the barrel and taking a bath in it."

"Count hands, Becka, and tell me how many people are hungry."

"I'll help count," said Biff. "We can both count to ten."

"I can count to one hundred." As the eldest child, Aaron felt intellectually superior to the twins.

"While you count, your mommy and I will go to the kitchen and get everything ready, okay? Let us know how many plates to fix."

The big country kitchen was in disarray, with dishes and partially prepared food on every visible surface. "It isn't as bad as it looks," Wynona said apologetically. "Everything is almost ready. We can finish up in ten minutes."

"Wynona, you shouldn't have gone to so much trouble for us," Sadie protested. "You've made yourself a nervous wreck over the food, and what really matters is that we get to be together."

"I know," Wynona muttered. "I should have stuck with a simple menu, and I would've if I'd known Melanie would pick tonight to be difficult." She gave Sadie an embarrassed grin. "It was jealousy, I guess. You outshine me in everything else, so I wanted to show off my cooking skills." She waved her hand at the cluttered countertops. "Aren't you impressed?"

Sadie went to Wynona and put an arm around her. "Don't you know that *I'm* jealous of *you*? You have these wonderful children, and a house of your own, and a fine marriage to a good man. You're so lucky, Wynona. As far as I'm concerned, it isn't fair that you should have all this and still be the best cook in Swisher County!"

There was a dazed expression on Wynona's face. "Do you really mean that?"

"Of course."

"But, Sadie, if that's what *you* want, all you have to do is snap your fingers and you can have it."

Sadie snapped her fingers. "I've been doing that for six years, and nothing has happened yet."

"Then I suggest you go out in the den and snap your fingers where Reese can hear you. He's yours for the asking, Sadie."

"Marriage to Reese isn't what I want. That would be a—well—a marriage of convenience, because we're both available and we've been friends for a long time. I want a marriage like yours, with someone to sweep me off my feet the way Tom did you. I want my husband to make me forget there are other men in the world, because he fills my heart so completely."

Wynona shook her head. "That isn't exactly the way it happened, Sadie."

"You were only engaged for two weeks."

Wynona nodded, but she seemed uncomfortable with the turn the conversation had taken. "Why don't you go take the men their beers?" she suggested. "And while you're out there, take a good look at Tom and ask yourself if he's the kind of man to sweep a woman off her feet. I love him more than I love my own life, and I wouldn't trade him for Indiana Jones or the Sundance Kid. But I had to learn to appreciate him."

Sadie carried the drinks into the den and mused on what Wynona had said. Maybe Sadie hadn't done a good job of explaining what she was searching for. She had discovered physical passion with Reese, but that wasn't the kind of excitement she meant. She wanted not only a physical mating but an emotional bonding with someone who needed her as much as she needed him. The kind of love she wanted grew from being needed desperately by someone else, the way Jerry Don had needed her. Reese needed nothing from her and in fact was usually on the giving end of their relationship. It was only when they were making love that she could give as fully as she received. She could marry Reese, but they couldn't make love *all* the time. And how they would spend the remainder sent terror through her being. She would have to become another person in order to find happiness with Reese, and she wasn't willing to give up her identity. For now, she would have to lavish her love on Sniffles.

"Did the kids ever settle down?" Wynona asked when she returned.

Sadie nodded. "There's a children's program on TV. They're caught up in some great cartoon adventure, and nobody's making a peep." She glanced around the kitchen and saw that order had been restored. "What's that I smell?" she asked, then looked with wonder at a magnificent standing-rib roast. On another platter was a smoked ham, beautifully decorated with pineapple slices and cherries. Sadie began to carry a never-ending procession of dishes to the dining-room table—salads and vegetables of every variety, both raw and cooked, relishes, and at least four kinds of homemade bread.

"I can't believe you didn't fry a chicken or bake a turkey," Sadie teased on her last trip.

Wynona's cheeks flamed crimson. "Would you settle for orange-glazed pheasant with wild rice stuffing?" She lifted the final dish from one of her three ovens. "Baked in a clay pot, of course."

Sadie gave Wynona an appraising glance. "Are you sure you weren't showing off for Reese instead of for me?"

"Of course not."

Sadie continued to speculate. "I know you once thought about marrying him. He talks about you all the time and about how lucky Tom is to be your husband. Maybe he's still carrying a torch for you."

Wynona was annoyed. "Don't be ridiculous. That was over a long time ago."

"It's been a long time since Jerry Don died, but I've been carrying a torch for him for six long years. You're right here in the same town with Reese and see him almost every day. It's probably a lot harder to forget under those circumstances."

When she would have continued, Wynona interrupted. "Sadie, I had a crush on him in high school, but that's all it ever was. Reese is very special to me, and he always will be. But he isn't in love with me now and probably never was. If you can't see for yourself that he's in love with *you*, then you're a whole lot dumber than I thought."

"He isn't in *love* with me, Wynona. He's in *lust* with me. That's something altogether different."

Tom wandered into the kitchen, munching on a carrot stick he'd picked up from the dining-room table. "What's this about lust?" he asked. "Are you women telling dirty jokes again?"

"Where's Melanie?" Wynona asked.

"Reese is holding her. She fell asleep, and he's afraid to put her down."

"Will you get the children to wash their hands while I put the baby to bed, then? Everything is ready as soon as we can get to the table."

She started from the kitchen, but Tom caught her and pulled her into his arms. "I believe you outdid yourself this time," he said admiringly. "I'm not sure that old table can hold up under the weight of all that food." He tilted her chin and briefly kissed her lips. "I'm real proud of you, darlin'."

Sadie felt like an interloper in a scene that was so casually intimate. With an unexpected heaviness in her heart, she slipped from the room. Never had she been so aware of what was lacking in her life.

Chapter Eleven

An only child herself, Sadie had never sat down to a family meal with the commotion created by several lively children. The twins and Aaron competed for adult attention by offering incredible tales of their daily adventures. With wide eyes, Becka told the story of the poisonous rattlesnake she'd discovered in the well house. "Daddy chopped it with a shovel," she said, "so it couldn't bite me."

Not to be outdone, Biff told of a giant snapping turtle that had mysteriously appeared in the stock tank, and Aaron related with gruesome details the birthing of a calf. There was little opportunity for adult conversation until the children finished eating and were ready for bed.

Sadie had to admire the other woman's organized household. Wynona served coffee and dessert to her husband and guests before excusing herself to draw water for three baths. Then, like a sentry on patrol, she moved from room to room, checking on each child before stopping by the dining room to chat with the adults. Over her objections, Sadie cleared the table and stacked the dishes in the dishwasher.

At last the children's day came to a close. They emerged from their baths sweet smelling and sleepy-headed, and when they came into the dining room to say good-night, they reached out in warm affection to pat Sadie's cheek. She realized with a wrenching sadness that she would miss them when she returned to Austin. She buried her face in Becka's blond curls and gave her an extra hug. When Sadie lifted her head, she had to wipe tears from her eyes.

"Carry me to bed, Daddy," Becka asked, opening her arms to her father. "I'm too tired to walk."

"Me, too," said Biff.

Tom picked up one child and Wynona took the other, leaving Aaron to walk.

"Come hold my hand," he said to Sadie. "I'm big, so you don't have to carry me. I have a room of my own, and I'm not even afraid in the dark."

Sadie reached for Reese's hand. "Would you like to come with us?"

They started down the hallway, Sadie and Reese on either side of Aaron. Reese stopped and knelt down beside Aaron. "I know you're a big boy," he said, tousling the boy's blond hair that was as straight and lustrous as strands of silk, "but I don't have a son of my own to carry to bed at night. Would you mind letting me carry *you* this time?"

"It's okay with me," Aaron answered. He held out his arms, and Reese lifted him in one easy swoop. Aaron clenched his hands around Reese's neck and snuggled against his chest with a contented smile on his face. "I'm big," he said, "but sometimes I like to get carried, too."

"I know, son, I know."

They went into Aaron's bedroom, and Sadie turned down the covers for him while Reese lowered him between the sheets. His room was surprisingly neat, with all the toys and games on their shelves and outdoor clothes on hooks. A large poster of Roger Staubach in his Dallas Cowboys football uniform was taped to the closet door.

"I'm going to play for the Dallas Cowboys someday," Aaron said sleepily. "I'm the best football player in my school." With that, he rolled over onto his stomach and buried his face in his pillow. Before Sadie and Reese reached the door, he was snoring softly.

When they returned to the den, Reese sat in the corner of the sofa and Sadie kicked off her sandals and nestled beside him, her bare feet tucked beneath her. Reese put his arm loosely across her shoulders and drew her closer to him, nuzzling her hair. During the brief time they were alone before Tom and Wynona rejoined them, they talked softly while their gazes clung and their hands strayed.

"You're a sweet man—do you know that?" Sadie's finger traced the crease at Reese's mouth, then contoured his lips.

He nipped her finger. "What makes you say so?" He closed his hand over hers and turned it so that her palm was open. He began kissing it, and when she smiled at him, he licked erotic circles.

She felt shivers of delight and squirmed against him. "How much longer do we have to stay here? I'm ready to go."

He licked the tip of each finger, then gave it a gentle bite. "I don't know what it is about that dress you're wearing," he said, "but it makes me feel like wanting to be an old-fashioned protector and at the same time to rip it off and ravish you." He touched the open buttons at the neckline, then brushed the eyelet-lace ruffle that peeked through. "Don't you know these two open buttons are an invitation to unbutton the rest of them?"

"Help yourself. It buttons all the way down the front."

"So you've turned into a tease, have you?" He grabbed the fabric as though to rip it open.

"Reese!" she squealed. "Don't!"

"Then quit being naughty, or you'll have no one but yourself to blame if Tom and Wynona walk in and find us making love on their sofa."

"I believe you'd do it," she said, laughing at his unexpected response. Reese had always been so conservative and self-controlled in his behavior. He'd never taken on the crazy dares that she and Jerry Don had found irresistible when they were young.

Reese drew her close and gave her a bear hug. Against the top of her head he whispered, "Time is running out. I have to take advantage of every opportunity you give me. So don't make an offer in public unless you're ready to carry it out."

"Why don't we go down to the volunteer fire station and ring the bell and invite the whole town to watch?"

He chuckled and relaxed his hold on her. "That should certainly satisfy everybody's curiosity."

Sadie gave him a speculative glance. "It might be kind of interesting. Have you ever made love in a fire truck before?"

"No, Sadie, but with you I think it would be a good idea to have a fire truck standing by so a flash fire won't get started and burn up the whole damn county."

Her cheeks reddened. "I'm not sure you meant it that way, but I think I'll take that as a compliment."

She leaned forward and would have kissed him, but they heard footsteps in the hallway. She quickly moved farther from Reese and straightened the neckline of her dress. As Tom and Wynona entered the room, Sadie realized that Reese's hand had slipped under the hem of her skirt and that he was toying with her bare feet. She managed to get one leg from beneath her and onto the floor, but he held tightly to her other foot and wouldn't let go. She shot him a pained expression, but he ignored it and assumed a cherubic grin.

She tried to carry on a normal conversation, but every time she responded to a remark, Reese would find a ticklish spot and feather it until her voice would squeak from the effort not to laugh. She finally lost all thread of the conversation and sat planning an appropriate revenge.

Fortunately her suffering was cut short. It was already well past Tom and Wynona's bedtime, and Tom's head began to droop.

"We need to go," Sadie said after an acceptable interval. "I'll be leaving at six in the morning, and I haven't even packed yet."

Startled into wakefulness, Tom asked, "How long before you come back to Tascosa, Sadie? Hope it won't be a whole year, like it was last time."

Sadie shook her head. She really didn't have an answer. It was one more thing she couldn't let herself think about. "Depends on how Mom gets along."

"It's been like old times to have you here for these two weeks," Wynona said, and talked about how much the children had enjoyed their daily playtime with Sadie.

"I'm really going to miss them," Sadie admitted. This visit had made her more keenly aware of how much she wanted children of her own. She would return to Austin with a new hollow place in her heart.

Her thoughts turned to the afternoon and her love-making with Reese. What would it be like to bear his child? The thought confused her and made her uneasy. She could accept the gift of their sexual passion, but only so long as it remained within its circumscribed bounds. Marriage to a man like Reese, who was self-sufficient and didn't need anything from anyone else, would be miserable for someone like Sadie, who needed to give herself totally.

Their visit ended with hugs and tears at the front door and repeated promises to do a better job of keeping in touch. Reese put his arm around Sadie's waist as they walked down the gravel driveway to his truck.

"Need my handkerchief?" he asked, offering it.

Sadie laughed through her tears. "You must buy these by the dozen."

He opened the door and lifted her up the high step into the truck. It was pitch-black except for the twinkling stars and a sliver of moon. Sadie took a deep breath and threw off her mood of dejection. The evening was not quite finished, and she had a score to settle.

Reese went around and got into the driver's seat, then started the engine. He let it idle for a moment and turned to Sadie, pulling her into his arms. He searched for her mouth and began a series of tiny kisses, evading her when her lips tried to cling. "Don't, Sadie," he whispered, "not unless you want to make love in Tom's driveway."

She drew her feet up under her so that she was kneeling on the seat, her head higher than Reese's, whose face was buried in the ruffles at her breast. He pushed the material aside and nuzzled her smooth skin with his chin. She bent her head and blew into his ear, then nipped gently at his earlobe. She moved her head downward, kissing along his neck until she could feel the pulse hammering in his throat.

"Let's get out of here," he said roughly, breaking away and gripping the steering wheel. "The blood in my veins turns to fire when you do that."

He backed the truck out of the driveway and onto the dirt road, then pulled Sadie close beside him and locked one arm around her. She lifted his hand to her lips and took little bites at the tips of his fingers. "I liked it when you did that to me," she said. She turned his hand to the fleshy part at the base of his thumb and nipped a little harder, then let her tongue draw circles along the creases of his palm.

They got to the stop sign at the crossroads, and Reese put the gearshift in park so that both hands were free to hold Sadie. He kissed her until they were breathless.

Lights from an approaching vehicle danced in the rearview mirror, and someone tooted a horn. "Everybody in the county knows my truck," Reese said. "It'll be all over town tomorrow that we were caught necking at the crossroads." He let the other car pass him and gave a nonchalant wave. The other driver tooted his horn again, as though in congratulation. Reese started to make a left turn toward Sadie's home, but she stopped him.

"I have something else in mind," she said. Her voice was full of mystery and promise. "Just follow my directions, and don't ask any questions."

She led him through a series of turns until they approached the northern edge of the tiny village of Tascosa. "Why on earth are we going into town?" Reese protested. "Everything has been closed for hours."

"Not *everything*." She directed him down one last street and into a driveway.

"Oh, no, Sadie! Not the fire station!"

"Can we get in?"

"I don't know. Someone may be on duty."

"An audience will make it even more interesting, won't it?"

He tilted his head and exploded with laughter. "I should have known you'd find a way to get even with me for playing footsie with you."

"Tell me again, Reese. Have you ever made love in a fire truck?"

"No, Sadie, I can honestly say the thought never even crossed my mind."

"But it does seem like a good idea now, right?"

"Wrong. I'm taking you home right now."

She wagged her finger at him. "If you do, you're going to be sorry."

"Why is that?"

"Because you won't get a good-night kiss—or anything else you might have been expecting."

"Sadie, you aren't serious about this, are you? You didn't really think we'd break into the fire station and make love there, did you?"

"You're so stuffy, Reese. Think of this as a chance to lighten up and let go of your ironclad self-discipline. Be spontaneous, can't you?" She gave him a seductive smile and wondered what he would do. Either way, she'd gotten her revenge. The expression of distress on his face right now was ample payment for the torture he'd inflicted upon her at the Evanses'.

He gave her an appraising glance. "You're on."

Sadie let out a hoot. "I never would have believed it! Straight Arrow has gone around the bend." She was sure he'd back out at the last minute, but she would push him to the limit. "Let's go."

Reese opened his door and stepped down, then helped Sadie out the same door. His hands lingered at her waist, then brushed against her breast, and she realized too late that he'd taken her dare believing that *she* would back out at the last minute. He intended to make the most of her folly, the scoundrel! Well, she would brazen it out. If they stopped short of their goal, it wouldn't be due to *her* cowardice. She put her hand over his and guided it to her neckline, then helped him unbutton one button. There were eight remaining. That should be enough to see her through the night.

The volunteer fire station was nothing more than a large sheet-metal shed with a domed roof and wide overhead doors for the fire truck to exit. An attached lean-to provided space for an office and sleeping area, though it was rarely put to use. One of the volunteer firemen was always on duty, but usually that meant only that any telephone calls to the station would automatically be routed to his home. The person on duty was expected to remain at home during his shift to be available if needed. Except during times of drought, when there was a constant risk of prairie fires, volunteers tended to use the station as a male gathering place for dominoes and gossip.

There were no lights on inside, but someone might be sleeping there. They wouldn't know until they tried the office door.

"It's locked," Reese said, moving around the corner to peek in the window. "It's too dark to see if anyone's inside."

"Where's the key?"

"Whoever is on duty will have it."

"That's a crazy idea. What if the other volunteers get to the station first? Does that mean they can't move the truck until the person on duty arrives?"

"Maybe they leave an extra key somewhere. I don't know. I'm not a regular volunteer. I live too far away."

They felt their way around the building in the darkness, looking for some way to get inside. There didn't seem to be any hiding place for a key.

"Now what?" Reese asked when it seemed their quest had ended in failure.

"I had my heart set on making love in that fire truck," she said with a woebegone sigh.

"Sadie, I'm not going to break the lock on that door, so don't give me that pleading look. I've managed to stay out of jail all these years, and I don't intend to do time for the county now."

"They wouldn't keep you more than two or three days. Wouldn't it be worth it?"

"With my luck, I'd get twenty years' hard time."

"Oh, well, forget that. I don't want them to lock you up for twenty years. I might want to snuggle up with you again sooner than that."

"I'm glad you've come to your senses. I'm ready to snuggle up right now." He put his arms around her and gave her a long, satisfying kiss. "Come on—let's get out of here."

Sadie lingered another moment. "You know, it just doesn't make sense that there isn't a key around here somewhere. They have to be able to get the fire truck out when the person on duty is late arriving." She went back around to the door of the office and searched for a hiding place. "Maybe if you drove your truck around here and shone the headlights, I'd be able to find something."

"No, Sadie. Somebody might drive past and notice us. We've created enough gossip tonight, as it is."

"You're such a prude, Reese. I had no idea." Sadie continued her walk around the building and ended where they'd started, with Reese's truck parked nearby.

"Give up?" he asked. "I'm game to hunt as long as you want, but you have to admit we could be making better use of our time." He gave her a coaxing smile and held out his arms to her.

"Oh, all right," she said, lifting her face for a kiss. When he pulled away, she asked, "Do you have a flashlight in your glove compartment?"

"You're the most stubborn female I've ever met," he grumbled. "You're more single-minded than that damned heifer I had to haul to the barn to keep it from starving! When you get something into your head—"

"Okay, okay." Sadie was properly chastened. "Let's go."

"No. I'm going to bring you the flashlight. *Then* we'll go."

"You don't have to sound so sore about it."

"I'm not *sore*, Sadie. I'm frustrated, damn it!"

"I've never seen you lose your temper before."

"I'm not losing my temper!" When he realized he was shouting, he apologized. "I guess what I'm losing is my sense of humor." He went to the truck and returned with a flashlight. "Here you go. You look all night if that's what you want to do. Wake me when you're ready to go home." He sank to the ground and leaned back against the building. "No hurry. Take your time."

"Are you trying to make me feel guilty?" she asked, scarcely able to hold back her laughter. Reese Chandler, who'd been born acting like a sexagenarian, was suddenly acting like a spoiled two-year-old. His stiff, unfailing self-control had vanished! She couldn't help twitting him a little. "You have to admit it would have been a lot of fun if it had worked out."

"Hell, yes. We could've had them take pictures for the newspaper, maybe even had it on television. You and me and a bright red fire truck with all the volunteer firemen squirting us down with a hose to put out the flames!"

"Don't forget the person who'd be ringing the fire bell."

"Oh, I figure you could do that yourself with one hand."

She giggled. "I suppose *you*'d be more interested in what I was doing with my other hand."

"Since you've lost interest in anything *I*'m interested in tonight, I imagine you'd use your other hand to wave at the cameras."

Sadie walked around the front of the building, flashing the light and trying not to laugh out loud. Poor Reese. She'd pushed his patience far enough. It was time to make amends. She finished the circle and rejoined him at the main part of the fire station. She sat down beside him and kissed his cheek. "No luck."

"You're absolutely convinced?"

She flashed the light along the bottom edge of the building. There were two metal handles at the base of the sliding garage door to lift it, with a lock centered between them. She focused the light on the lock, but there was no key in it. Curiosity made her get up and move closer, and on an impulse she grabbed hold of the metal handle and gave it a tug.

The overhead door flew upward.

"Reese, the door isn't even locked! Come on—we can get inside!"

"Well, I'll be damned" was all he could say.

He helped her push up the door enough for them to crawl underneath and then slid it back down on its pulley. Sadie aimed the flashlight around the garage. "Oh, my," she said, "isn't that the most beautiful red fire truck you ever saw?"

It was candy-apple red and polished to a beautiful glossy sheen. Sadie started to step on the running board and hesitated. "The paint is so perfect, I'm afraid I'll scratch it if I touch anything."

"Wait here," Reese said. "I'll go see if there are some blankets in the bunk room." The engine room was totally dark when he left with the flashlight, and Sadie was glad when she heard his footsteps returning. He folded one blanket and stretched it across the running board, then stood on that to spread other blankets over the seat and door. "Here you go," he said, lifting her lightly over the door and onto the back seat. When she was settled, he handed her the flashlight while he vaulted over the door.

"No fingerprints," Sadie said. "We don't want to leave a trace."

He sat down beside her and pulled her into his arms. "You got your wish. Let's make the most of it."

The flashlight rolled onto the floor of the truck, its light beaming eerily in the heavy darkness. Reese found the ruffles of Sadie's dress more by feel than by sight, and undid the buttons so hurriedly that one of them popped off and bounced off the seat. "I'll find it later," he whispered while his hands kept busy with the eyelet-lace camisole. "How do you get this thing off?" he demanded.

Sadie lifted her arms and he jerked the camisole over her head, then fumbled with her petticoat until it was freed to join her other garments on the front seat. She was clad only in thin silk panties, and he eased those down her hips, then laid her backward on the blanket-lined leather seat. He knelt beside her, using his hands and mouth to ignite the fires of her passion until she writhed and moaned and begged him for release. The heat built inside her and reached a crescendo, holding her tense and taut and unsatisfied, her nerve endings thrumming like wires stretched too tight. Blindly she reached for Reese, who was both the creator and the fulfillment of her desire. Despite her pleas, he evaded her hands when she would have drawn him close, removed his clothes, and urged him inside her. Instead, he kept her trembling at the brink in order to intensify her ecstasy.

When she arched her back and cried out his name, he worked his magic with her until her heat concentrated in one place, became liquid fire, and melted outward from the core of her being with a dizzying explosion. Spasms swept through her, and he kissed her over and over until she lay spent, her body soaked with sweat.

"Reese," she whispered. "Oh, Reese, what did you do to me? I never dreamed a woman could have such feelings."

"There's more," he answered. "There's so much more, Sadie. Let me show you."

And then he took off his clothes, and though he began with exquisite tenderness, she responded with total abandonment. She was as eager to give pleasure as to receive it, and she followed the lead of his hands and lips like an inspired student. They used their bodies as instruments of mutual bliss, each technique or position offering possibilities for further experimentation and enjoyment. Time was their ally instead of their enemy, for they felt no need to hurry. Leisurely they partook of each other, seeking out particular delights and letting their passion build slowly.

"Reese..." The fires were once again rising in Sadie.

He pressed her face between his hands and kissed her lips.

"Please..."

He slipped his tongue between her lips and began to stroke the roof of her mouth, the sides of her tongue. When she began to sigh softly, he buried his lips in the sweet hollow of her neck, teasing until she shivered with thrilling sensations. When he reached her sensitive breasts, she dug her fingernails into his back and thought she would dissolve with pleasure. Somehow he knew she was ready and entered her, his own passion so great now that his control was almost gone.

Fiercely he thrust into her, and then they locked in a mating rhythm as old as time itself. Passion, once ignited, became all-consuming in its fiery demands, and what had begun in tenderness ended in a blazing inferno that melted them from the inside out and left them fused together for eternity.

"You're wonderful," Reese whispered, brushing Sadie's lips with his own.

She sighed and stretched lazily against him. "So are you."

They kissed again, with the gentle warmth that lingers after passion's raging fires have been spent.

"We need to go."

Sadie curled into a ball. "I'm too sleepy. Let's stay here all night."

Reese reached toward the front seat of the fire truck and groped for his clothes. "Where's the flashlight?" he asked, then found it under the blanket. He shone it into Sadie's face. "You're beautiful. Do you know that?"

Sadie's lips curved into a smile. "Thank you." She opened her arms to him. "Come here."

He shook his head. "No, ma'am. I recognize that look in your eye, and we've got to get out of here before someone catches us."

"Oh, Reese. Everybody is sound asleep. Nothing is going to stir in Tascosa until the sun comes up."

Reese pulled on his clothes, then nudged Sadie. "Come on, sweetheart. Let me help you get dressed."

He seemed to be at a loss what to do with all the ruffled undergarments. "Does this go on first?" he asked.

She sat up and reached for her petticoat. "Maybe I ought to tie this to the fire-truck antenna as a trophy," she said before wiggling herself into it. She put on the camisole he handed her. "Don't you want to help me with this?" she asked, leaning forward and dangling its narrow satin ribbons at him. "You can tie the bow for me."

He handed her the flashlight and fumbled with the ribbons while Sadie sat breathless and still, her breasts high and firm beneath his fingers. When he had finished, he took a deep, shaky breath, then buried his face in her softness. "Yes, you're beautiful, and yes, I want you—"

Sadie stretched her limbs like a cat being stroked.

"And no, we're not staying here another minute." Reese forced himself away from Sadie and handed her dress to her.

She gave a soft wail of protest. "But, Reese, I'm leaving in a few hours. This is our last chance."

"Don't remind me." His voice was bitter. He beamed the flashlight around the floor of the fire truck. "I can't find your button."

Sadie sensed that mention of their parting had affected Reese's mood. His face was sullen in the dim light, and he seemed angry. These sudden mood shifts were part of their old relationship, but Sadie had never understood them. Their old conflicts and misunderstandings might have been due to undercurrents of sexual tension between them, she realized. Even when she'd been most in love with Jerry Don, had she felt sexually attracted to Reese? The idea was too troubling to contemplate.

"I think it rolled under the seat." While Reese bent down to look for the missing button, Sadie slipped into her dress and sandals.

"Here it is." Reese handed her the button, and she tucked it into her pocket.

"I thought you'd want to keep it as a souvenir," she said, giving him a teasing smile. She was determined to do something to brighten his mood and chase away the storm clouds that loomed threateningly over their parting.

"I have my souvenir," Reese said, turning serious. "The smell of you, the taste of you. You're in my pores, Sadie. I won't need a button to remind me of the way you felt in my arms."

"Reese, don't." He was moving into uncharted waters, and Sadie was frightened. Her pulse hammered, and she felt a lump in her throat.

"Don't what? Don't tell you I'll never forget this day as long as I live? Don't tell you that I'll never hear a mockingbird or see a fire truck again without thinking of you? Don't tell you that every night I'll dream of you and my arms will reach out for you?" His voice had risen steadily, and Sadie put her head between her hands, trying to stave off the force of his words. "Don't tell you that I *love you*, damn it!"

"No, Reese, don't! Don't say it. It isn't true."

"It is true, Sadie. It's always been true."

She shook her head. "No," she whimpered. "You and I were *friends*, Reese. It was Jerry Don who *loved* me. And I loved *him*."

Reese smacked his fist against the seat. "Why can't you face the truth, Sadie? Why won't you accept the fact that I love you?"

"Because you don't love me the way Jerry Don did," she said, her voice so muffled by tears that she was almost incoherent. "And that's the kind of love I have to have. Your kind of love would destroy me!"

Reese flinched from some deep inner pain. Then the emotional storm ended as quickly as it had begun. He reached for his handkerchief and wiped any telltale fingerprints from the glossy chrome and bright paint of the fire truck, then carefully refolded the blankets he'd brought from the bunk room. Without a word he lifted Sadie over the side of the truck and checked to be certain that everything was in order.

He flashed the light around the dark fire station. "Everything the same way it was when we came in?" he asked.

Sadie nodded without speaking. The only thing that had changed was themselves.

Chapter Twelve

The loud, metallic banging of garbage cans being emptied into the city trash truck disturbed Sadie's sleep long before her alarm clock buzzed. She turned over and buried her face in her pillows, trying unsuccessfully to muffle the noise. Gradually she became fully awake and, with consciousness, totally unhappy.

Though it was only five o'clock, she swung her feet over the side of her bed and got up. She wouldn't lie here, feeling sorry for herself and getting more depressed, before the day had even started. She went through her morning chores with a determined cheerfulness, trying to force her lips into a smile. This had been her routine for the past week since she'd returned to Austin. It was the way she braced herself emotionally for the anguish of the day to come.

She could hear water running in the shower in the apartment next door, and from the other direction she could hear someone's stereo playing. To the east of her was the constant roar of traffic on the interstate. Why hadn't she noticed before how noisy her apartment complex was?

She went into her tiny kitchen and made a cup of instant coffee in the microwave and poured a glass of frozen orange juice. For a moment she toyed with the idea of scrambling herself an egg. She had worlds of time before she had to leave for work. But then she remembered the golden omelet Reese had brought her on a breakfast tray the last morning she was in Tascosa, and she lost all appetite. She would wait until she got to work. Maybe if somebody went to the cafeteria and kept her company, she'd be able to eat.

She was an hour early when she arrived at work, wearing a new, bright blue print summer dress with a white jacket. She thought she was the first one in her department, but someone called out to her as she went toward her cubicle.

"Hey, Sadie."

She turned to wave at her tall, good-looking colleague, Vince Schachter. Charming and self-confident, he was considered the agency's most eligible bachelor. "Oh, hi, Vince. Did you just get back from vacation?"

"Yeah, at four o'clock this morning. I figured I'd better not go to bed or I'd never make it to the office this morning." He gave his hilarious version of a Caribbean cruise, followed by a description of his return flight from Miami to Dallas with several of his newfound friends. "I missed the last plane to Austin," he admitted with a laugh. "I had to rent a car in Dallas and drive home."

"Sounds like you had yourself quite a time."

"Yeah. The phone was ringing in my apartment when I walked in this morning. The Dallas bunch is coming to Austin this weekend to see me." Vince leaned against a file cabinet and gave Sadie a grin. "How come my charm never worked on you, Sadie? I can knock 'em dead from here to Nassau, but you just give me that disinterested look and walk on by."

"I didn't want to give you a chance to break another heart." She gave him a friendly wave and went on to her cubicle. There were a dozen phone calls she needed to return before she could finish writing up her reports, and she needed to get some information about certification requirements from another department. Wasn't there something she could start on *now*, so she could get her mind busy and keep from thinking about personal matters that would only make her miserable? She reached for a big stack of computer printouts. She had to do comparison checks and transfer data. It was the most mind-numbing job in the department.

Eventually eight o'clock approached and other people began to wander in. There were the usual morning greetings and exchanges about the previous evening's activities. "Do we need another pot of coffee already?" asked their harried supervisor, already on the way to a conference. "Sadie, will you sit in on this meeting with me?" she asked. "You were the one who wrote the report, and there may be some questions."

The morning passed, typical of any other morning since Sadie had gone to work at the agency. She liked the people she worked with and had always been popular with them. She had always thought of her colleagues as friends, but today she realized that her ties with these people she spent so much time with amounted to nothing more than superficial acquaintanceship. They didn't really know her, and she didn't really know them. There was not one of them in whom she would dare confide about Reese. Never in her life had she more desperately needed a true friend; and never had one been so unavailable.

She returned from a second conference and glanced at her watch. Almost noon.

"How about lunch?" asked Vince. "Want to walk over to Scholz's? Cynthia and Tyson have already gone."

Sadie thought of the big portions of food served at Scholz's, a historic beer garden and landmark Austin institution located a few blocks away. She didn't have enough appetite for a Scholz blue-plate special. On the other hand, she didn't want to eat alone today. "Scholz's is fine," she said.

The July humidity stood at almost ninety percent, and Sadie was wilted by the time they'd walked three blocks. "I don't think I'll ever get used to the sweltering Austin summers," she said. "It's hot in the Panhandle, but at least it's dry, and there's always a breeze."

"Does that mean you want to sit inside in the airconditioning, instead of out in the beer garden?" There was a crowd at the popular restaurant, and they would have to wait for an inside table. Everybody wanted the comfort of air-conditioning today.

Sadie shook her head. It didn't matter. They went around to the back and sat down at a picnic table in the shade of a huge oak tree. Starlings were squawking overhead, and there was the noise of car motors and squealing brakes from the busy streets on either side of the restaurant.

"Peaceful out here, isn't it?" Vince said after the waitress had taken their order.

"Peaceful?" Sadie asked in surprise. Compared to what? she wondered. Certainly not compared to Tascosa, and the hidden creek that ran through Reese's ranch, and the soft trill of mockingbirds, or the gentle murmur of cottonwood leaves in the ever-present wind.

"You know, everybody having a good time, laughing and talking," Vince said. "Yeah, peaceful." He reached for her hand. "Something wrong?" he asked. "You seem awfully quiet today."

"Do I? I guess I'm just busy. I've been on vacation, too, and now I'm trying to catch up."

"Where'd you go?" he asked. "Did you take that backpacking trip in the Rockies you'd been planning?"

"No, my mom broke her leg," Sadie explained. "I had to go home and take care of her for a while."

"Too bad it spoiled your vacation. Maybe you can go backpacking next month." He gave her an appraising glance. "If you'll wait till after payday, I'll go with you."

They were interrupted by the arrival of the waitress with their orders.

"Now, about the backpacking trip—"

"Vince, no. I'm not going this year. I've got to stick close to a telephone in case my mom needs me again."

"Then let's start with something smaller. How about going sailing on Town Lake tomorrow after work?"

Sadie was about to say no, but she thought about the long, endless nights since she'd come back to Austin. Anything would be better than another evening by herself. "Okay."

Vince didn't try to hide his surprise. "After two years you finally said yes to a date?" he asked. "What changed your mind?"

Sadie had no intention of admitting her loneliness. She grinned at him. "Curiosity, I guess."

* * *

"How are you feeling tonight, Mom?" Sadie asked her mother on the telephone. She'd been calling home every evening for an update.

"Just fine, dear. Al took me into town to do some shopping today. I'm getting around fine on one crutch now. What about you, dear? How are things at work?"

"Not much change. A guy I work with came back from vacation yesterday. We're going sailing on Town Lake this evening."

"Sadie, you haven't mentioned a boyfriend to me. Who is he?"

"He's not a boyfriend, Mom. He's just a guy in my department."

"How old is he?"

"Oh, early thirties, I suppose." Sadie paused. She could almost hear the wheels turning in her mother's brain. "And yes, Mom, he's good-looking, too. And single."

"Is he better looking than Reese?" Nelda sounded peeved.

"Umm, hard to say. He's a little taller, but not so rugged through the shoulders. He's got dark, curly hair, though, and a cute dimple in one cheek."

"I'm sure he's conceited, then."

"As a matter of fact, he's not. He's a heck of a nice guy, and everybody likes him. He's got a personality kind of like Jerry Don's—you know, easygoing and full of fun. He's always the life of the party."

"What's his name?"

Sadie covered the receiver with one hand to hide her laughter. Her mother had asked for Vince's name as though she might have to engrave it on a wedding invitation.

"Vince Schachter. Do you want me to spell it for you?"

"Never mind. I think you've spoken of him before."

"I probably have. He's been on my monitoring team pretty often."

"You mean when you travel?"

"Yes, Mom. We travel the whole state together. Isn't that shocking?"

"It certainly wasn't done in my day." Nelda's disapproval was palpable. "Reese was by this afternoon and asked about you, dear."

Now it was Sadie who was being tweaked. She squirmed uncomfortably, then answered, "That's nice."

"Shall I give him a message from you, dear?"

"No, Mom. We said everything there was to say the last time we saw each other."

"I don't understand, dear."

"I'm sure you don't, but I'm not interested in explaining it to you." Her emotions were still too raw to allow anyone to probe, least of all a strong-willed mother with a single-option plan for Sadie's life. "I've got to run, Mom. Vince will be here any minute, and

I need to grab my swimsuit. I'll call you tomorrow night, okay?''

"Call me Saturday morning, dear. Al is taking me to play bingo tomorrow night.''

Sadie stretched out on the deck of Vince's day sailer and allowed the heat of the late-afternoon sun to relax her tense muscles. Behind her, Vince sat in the cockpit and stretched the sheet, then held the tiller until the boat began to drift with the current. When they got out in the middle of the lake, he reached into the compartment for the chilled wine coolers he'd brought along.

"Have a drink,'' he said, balancing carefully to hand her the bottle.

Sadie trailed one hand in the water for a while, then gingerly worked her body so she was lying on her back rather than her stomach.

While the sailboat drifted, they chatted about their work, their colleagues, movies and books—general topics they'd explored many times before on monitoring trips—but nothing of a personal nature. "Want to trade places?'' Sadie asked when she saw she was starting to turn pink.

"Are you prone to sunburn?'' Vince asked, easing himself into her spot on the deck as they exchanged places.

She shook her head. "Not usually. Tomorrow I should be nice and brown.''

"I'm brown, too, but I have to work at it," Vince replied. "I spend the winter in a tanning booth so I won't blister and peel when summer comes." He had a movie-star tan that looked fantastic contrasted against his white trunks. Sadie was surprised at his candor in telling how he'd gotten to look that way. Somehow she'd expected Vince to be the kind of guy who'd try to impress a woman, but he was completely natural and unassuming with her.

She wondered if she could talk to Vince, really talk to him. He seemed so approachable, and she was so desperate to talk to someone about Reese. She was still as confused as she'd been when she left Tascosa, and she couldn't sort out her feelings, because she hadn't been able to express them in words and force them into making some kind of sense. She took another sip of her wine cooler and watched the sky turn pink and lavender.

The wind shifted on the lake, catching the sail and sending the boom flying past Sadie. She grabbed for the sheet but she was too slow; the Dolphin flipped over and sent them tumbling into the water.

Vince came up splashing and laughing. "Are you okay?"

Sadie swam up beside him and helped him tilt the boat upright. "I wasn't paying attention," she confessed. "I'm sorry."

"No problem. It happens at least once every trip." He helped her back into the cockpit and scrambled in beside her, tugging at the sheet line while Sadie worked the boom. They turned the boat and sailed back toward the shore where Vince's car was parked. With the new breeze, the return trip was much faster, and it was barely dark when they arrived at the dock.

"Want to drop anchor for a while?" he asked. "Or shall we get dressed and go have dinner?"

"I'm enjoying this, if you are."

"Sure. We can eat later." He waved at a friend with a noisy group onshore, then dropped the anchor. "What's on your mind, Sadie?" he asked, sitting down beside her in the cramped cockpit.

Sadie was feeling a little awkward now. Somehow she'd expected to ease her way into this conversation, not have to blurt it out. Maybe this wasn't such a hot idea, after all.

Vince reached into the compartment and pulled out another wine cooler for each of them. "Here," he said. "Settle back in the dark and tell me all about it."

"You're sure you don't mind?"

"What are friends for?" When she remained silent, he added, "Look, Sadie, I may not be able to help, but you obviously need to talk to somebody. You keep people at a distance with that sunshiny way of yours that spreads a little warmth on everybody but doesn't let anybody get close enough to know you. You're probably as close to me as you are to anyone, so why not tell me what's on your mind? Take a chance and trust somebody, for once."

She stretched out her hands in mute appeal. "I'm afraid to trust anybody," she said. "I can't even trust myself."

Vince took her by the shoulders and made her look at him. The lights along the shore glimmered and bounced against the water and reflected in his eyes. Sadie saw nothing but sympathy and concern in his expression. "Look, Sadie, *I'm* trusting *you*," he said softly. "I'm trusting you enough to let you tell me something that may be as painful for me to hear as it is for you to tell. I'm trusting you not to hate me after you tell me something you've kept festering inside you for a long time. I'm trusting you to be honest with both of us about something that's important. If I can trust you that much, then *you* can trust *me*. I'm taking just as big a risk as you are."

"I never thought of it that way before," she said in wonderment, and then she began to tell Vince the whole story of Jerry Don and Reese and Wynona....

"So that's the way it is," she said finally. "I'm so attracted to Reese he drives me wild, but I don't love him. I *can't* love him. Not ever. What I feel for him is too mixed up with what I felt for Jerry Don. I betrayed Jerry Don, and he's been haunting me ever since."

"You know what I think, Sadie?" Vince said thoughtfully. "I think it's no wonder you're afraid to let yourself love a man. You felt guilty over what happened between you and Reese that day, and when you learned about Jerry Don's death, it seemed like a punishment you somehow deserved."

"Oh, surely that's not it," she protested.

"Then why have you run away from Reese for a second time?"

"You mean last week? I didn't. It was time to come back to Austin."

"Be honest with yourself, Sadie. When he told you he loved you, you rejected him. You said you didn't even kiss him goodbye."

"I didn't run away," she muttered. "We were at an impasse with nothing left to say."

"Have you talked to him since you came back?"

"No, and I'm not going to. It's over, and it needs to stay that way."

"If it's really over, why are you afraid to talk to him?"

"I'm not *afraid*, for heaven's sake. I just don't want to argue with him anymore."

"What if Reese weren't in the picture?" Vince asked. "What would you do about the principal's job in Tascosa?"

Sadie pondered the question. "I don't know," she admitted at last. "I'm ready to settle down and quit all this traveling. I'd like to have someplace where I belong again. I feel like such a misfit now. When I was in Tascosa I kept wishing I were in Austin, and now that I'm here, I keep wishing I were back in Tascosa." She gave a deep sigh. "But Reese *is* in the picture there, and it's more complicated than I can deal with. I'll wait for another job. Something else will come along that's right for me."

Vince gathered up the empty bottles and stowed them in a duffel bag. "You're worn-out," he said gently. "I'm going to take you home so you can get some rest tonight. We'll talk some more after you've had a few days to think things over, okay?"

Sadie reached out for his hand and gripped it hard. "Thanks for listening."

"Any time." He stood and helped her onto the dock, then pulled anchor and together they got the boat onto the trailer attached to Vince's car. When he left Sadie at her apartment door, he kissed her cheek. They said good-night, and as Vince turned to go, he said in puzzlement, "You know, one thing I can't understand is how Wynona fits into all this."

"Wynona? She's my best friend."

"So if she's your friend, why couldn't you confide in her? Why did you have to come to me?"

"I didn't want to talk to *Wynona* about my mixed-up feelings for Jerry Don and Reese," Sadie answered emphatically.

"I realize that," Vince replied. "But what I don't understand is why."

Chapter Thirteen

For the next several days, Sadie pondered her conversation with Vince, oftentimes with great discomfort. He'd been a psychologist before coming to work at the agency, and his background had trained him to probe human emotions. In one session he'd helped her discover truths about herself that she'd resisted for years, and she was drained by the experience. Yet, even as she exhausted herself from the struggle to know the truth, she felt an inner cleansing that energized her and gave her new courage and hope.

She remembered what her mother had said about withdrawing into a cocoon when Sadie's father had died. Sadie had done the same thing when Jerry Don had died, she now realized. For six years she'd been enshrouded like a forming caterpillar. Now, perhaps, she would be able to emerge from that living tomb and soar like a butterfly—if only she kept faith with herself.

"How about a drink after work tonight?" Vince asked, stopping by Sadie's cubicle in midafternoon. It had been almost a week since their sailboat ride on Town Lake, and their only contact during the interval had been casual and work related.

"I'd like that." Their eyes met, and Sadie gave him a warm smile.

"You know, you're a lot prettier with a real smile instead of one of those artificial ones like you used to flash around here."

Sadie gave a wry chuckle. "My razzle-dazzle cheerleader smile? I couldn't get along without it before."

"It may have fooled a lot of people, but it didn't fool me."

"Do you know *all* my secrets? What are you? A magician or something?"

"Nothing magic about it," he answered. "Nothing but careful observation and scientific deduction. Of course, having three sisters helps." He gave her a jaunty wave. "I'll stop by at five o'clock."

Sadie was so busy the rest of the afternoon, she scarcely had time to look up. Just before five her telephone rang, and the receptionist said she had a visitor.

"Oh, all right," she said with irritation. It never failed that when she had plans for after work, something unexpected would detain her. She gathered up her purse and put it on the corner of her desk. Maybe her visitor would take a not-too-subtle hint.

"Second door on your left," came the receptionist's voice. Footsteps sounded on the carpeted hallway and hesitated. Sadie turned, an automatic smile on her face.

The smile crumpled. "Reese!"

"Hello, Sadie." He stood in the doorway, looking almost more uncomfortable than she was.

Sadie quickly took in his navy blazer and khaki slacks. Gone was the cowboy in jeans and plaid shirt, to be replaced by this stranger, who looked like any other prosperous, handsome businessman. Her heart started pounding furiously. She'd told herself to forget him. But could she? Something made her want to go to him and put her arms around him, but she fought the urge. "Come in," she said, indicating an armchair and moving to her own chair behind her desk.

He remained standing, but Sadie's knees were weak from the shock he'd given her. She sat down, then realized he was towering over her. His very presence dominated her tiny cubicle.

"So this is your office?" he said, turning to take in the whole thing.

"Such as it is."

He cleared his throat. "Smaller than I expected."

"Yes. Well, I don't spend much time here. I'm usually traveling."

The silence lengthened, gathering tension. Then they both spoke at once.

"What brings—"

"I thought—"

Sadie lifted her gaze and saw that there were shadows under Reese's eyes, and his expression had taken on a new uncertainty. What had happened to his legendary self-assurance?

Someone came down the hallway, whistling. "Ready to go, Sadie?" Vince stuck his head in the door, then drew back in surprise. "Excuse me," he said. "I didn't know you had company."

"It's okay, Vince. I'd like you to meet Reese Chandler, an old friend from Tascosa. Reese, this is Vince Schachter. We work together."

Vince thrust out his hand, and a little slowly, perhaps, Reese responded. The two men stood sizing each other up, with Sadie momentarily forgotten as she watched the interchange between them. Vince kept his friendly smile, though he must have been about to burst with curiosity. But Reese betrayed his hostility in the way he clenched his jaw.

"Sadie and I were about to go have a drink," Vince said, still cordial. "Would you care to join us?"

Reese turned to Sadie, a pained expression on his face. It was obvious that the last thing on earth he wanted was to spend another minute in the company of Vince Schachter. "I'm only in town for a few hours—on business."

"That's too bad," Vince responded. "Maybe another time." Grinning at Sadie, he asked, "Shall we go?"

"Excuse me," Reese interrupted. "Could I have a minute with Sadie?"

"Be my guest. I'll step outside." Vince made his exit, but there were no retreating footsteps, and it was clear that he was waiting just outside the door.

"Sadie, I've got to talk to you," Reese insisted.

"Then why don't you come have a drink with us, and we can talk afterward?"

"No, there isn't time before the next plane back."

"Can't you take a later plane, then?"

"No, damn it. I have to talk to you *now*."

"I don't want to talk to you, Reese. We've said everything there is to say. All we'll accomplish is to hurt each other."

"I'm not going to hurt you, Sadie. I have to know how you're doing."

"I'm fine, Reese. Can't you tell?"

Reese slammed one fist against his other, open palm with a loud smack. "Tell him you can't go tonight," he demanded. "Now. Tell him."

Sadie felt herself weakening under the force of his will, but stubborn pride held her back. She sat paralyzed with indecision.

Just at that moment, Vince popped back inside her office. "You know, it just occurred to me that you two might have some catching up to do. Why don't we take a rain check for tomorrow night, Sadie?"

Reese managed to wipe the scowl off his face and give Vince a curt nod. Sadie gave him a limp smile of gratitude. As she braced herself for a stormy evening, Vince sauntered down the hall, whistling.

Sadie and Reese sat on the crowded patio at the Lakeview Café, staring alternately at their drinks and across the road to the lake. "Can I bring you anything else?" asked their waitress. "Nachos?"

"I'm not hungry, thanks," Sadie said when Reese glanced in her direction.

"Let me know if you change your mind." The waitress gave Reese a friendly smile before bouncing off to an adjoining table.

"How can she move so fast in this humidity?" Reese said. "It's all I can do to breathe, the air's so heavy."

"That's July in Austin for you. Sweltering." Sadie stole a glance at Reese. He really did look uncomfortable in his coat and tie. "Why don't you take off your jacket?"

There was the merest flicker of a smile on Reese's lips. "After all the money I spent to impress you, too. I might as well have worn my jeans." He shrugged off the blazer and laid it across a chair back, then loosened the knot in his tie and rolled up his shirt sleeves. "That's better," he said, taking a sip of his drink. "Now we can get down to business."

"What business?" They'd said almost nothing for the past half hour, each of them waiting for the other to take the initiative. Apparently Reese had grown impatient with the waiting game. Sadie felt the muscles in her abdomen tighten and braced herself for the worst. She had no idea what to expect from Reese at this point.

"Two things," he answered. "I came to see if you're happy, and I came to offer you a job."

"I'm happy, and I have a job. I guess that takes care of your business." Sadie leaned back with a scowl and dared him to argue with her.

The twist of Reese's lips was just as belligerent. "This isn't any easier for me than it is for you, you know."

"I didn't ask you to come here and barge into my life."

"I didn't ask you to come back to Tascosa and remind me of almost forgotten dreams, either. But you did, Sadie—and nothing will ever be the same again." His voice was so low she had to strain to hear his final words.

"It isn't my fault, Reese. It just happened, that's all. Blame Mom's garden hose if you have to blame something. We had our moment and it's over. Life goes on."

"I'm glad you can be so fatalistic," he said sarcastically. "I should've known you'd run like you always do when you start to have any feelings."

Sadie opened her lips to disagree until it occurred to her that there was something familiar about what he'd said. Run from her feelings? Wasn't that what Vince had accused her of doing, too? Surely they were wrong about her—weren't they? "That's not fair, Reese. I've spent the past six years feeling so much pain I've been numb."

"You mean you've spent six years wallowing in pain and making a career out of it so you wouldn't ever have to get close to anyone again. You've kept your distance so you wouldn't have to risk getting hurt."

Sadie flinched at his cold fury. "If that's what I intended, I was certainly mistaken," she said, gazing at the tabletop to avoid his merciless scrutiny. "I got close to *you*, and I've been hurting ever since." She felt her lip begin to tremble and bit until she tasted blood. She refused to let herself cry in Reese's presence again. She would end this ordeal with dignity if it killed her. "If you don't mind," she said when she'd regained control of her voice, "I'd like to go now. I'll drop you at the airport if you'd like."

"Sadie, don't," Reese said, reaching for her hand when she attempted to rise. "This isn't going the way I planned. I didn't come here to fight with you. I don't know what's the matter with me. I'm so mixed-up I can't even think straight anymore." He buried his face in his hands. Sadie's heart went out to him.

She stroked the muscle along his neck and shoulder.

He gripped her hand in his and slowly shook his head. "Can we go somewhere else to talk?" he asked. "I still haven't said what I came here to say."

"It's time to go to the airport if you're going to make your plane."

He signaled for their check. "I'll go back tomorrow."

If they were going to have a private conversation, there was really no choice but for Sadie to take Reese home with her. She drove to the concrete jungle of apartment complexes and ushered Reese into the tiny apartment she had rented two years ago because it had a patio overlooking the Colorado River and stately live-oak trees in the courtyard. Otherwise it was an ordinary, garden-variety apartment—functional but without personality or style.

"How about some iced tea?" Sadie asked. She went to the thermostat and turned on the air-conditioning, then flipped the switch for the overhead fan. The living room had got hot during the afternoon but would soon cool off.

"Anything is fine." Reese followed her into the kitchen while she poured the tea, then went back to the living room and chose an armchair across from the sofa.

"I'll be out in a minute," Sadie called. "I'm going to change into my shorts. Turn on the TV if you'd like." She went into her bathroom and splashed cold water on her face while she considered the situation she was in. Reese seemed to be as tense as she was, yet determined to have his say. Obviously he intended to talk to her about the principal's job in Tascosa, and obviously she was going to refuse it. They'd been at that same stalemate two weeks ago when she'd left Tascosa. So why had he gone to all the trouble to come to Austin?

She went into the living room, carrying Sniffles. "Do you recognize Sniffles?" she said. "Hasn't he grown?" She offered him to Reese for inspection, then sat down on the sofa and cuddled the rabbit in her lap, rubbing his neck.

"He must have culture shock," Reese said with a smile. "This city apartment doesn't bear much resemblance to that wheat furrow where I found him."

"At least he's safe from hawks here."

"I have to admit he seems to be thriving."

"Some creatures do better in the city than in the country."

"Are you talking about Sniffles?"

"I'm talking about me."

"Is that your final answer?"

Sadie hesitated. "I'm not sure what the question is."

Reese leaned forward, intensity giving an edge to his voice. "Sadie, some members of the school board want you to apply for the principal's job. They want someone who can take over the migrant grant and get the program rolling in September, and they think you're the best person for the job. They sent me to see if you'd come for a formal interview next Saturday afternoon."

"Reese, we've been through this before. You know what my answer is."

"Let me finish. I told them how you feel, but they think you might change your mind."

She shook her head. "I don't belong in Tascosa anymore, Reese."

"Then where do you belong, Sadie?"

Her eyes filled with tears. "I don't know. I used to think I belonged in Austin, but ever since I came back, I've felt out of place here, too. I don't seem to belong anywhere now."

Reese reached out to touch her hand, then folded it within his palm. "I came to see if you were happy in Austin, Sadie. I wanted to see the place where you work, and where you live. I promised myself that if you seemed happy, I wouldn't say anything about your coming back to Tascosa."

"I *am* happy," she insisted.

"Look me in the eye and tell me the truth, Sadie. You grew up as free as the wind on the plains, and now you're living in acres of concrete and working in a space you couldn't even turn a pony in. Your apartment is about as homey as a motel, and there's so much noise you can't hear yourself think. Is this what you want out of life? If you can say that and mean it, I won't say another word."

She hugged Sniffles to her breast and didn't answer.

"Are you happy, Sadie?"

She shrugged. "Sometimes. Happy enough, I guess."

"You deserve better than that, Sadie. Why settle for so little?"

"Would it be any different in Tascosa?" she asked.

"I think it might be," Reese said softly. "You've already faced up to most of your demons in Tascosa. I'm the only one you've got left."

"You're the one I can't deal with, Reese. You keep me so confused I don't know what I think or how I feel."

He moved over to the sofa and sat down beside her. "Are you sure you don't know how you feel?" He put his hand on her chin and lifted her face, gazing deeply into her eyes.

"I won't deny the desire I have for you," she said. "But, Reese, we can't be happy with a relationship that's based on nothing but sexual attraction. We'd only be using each other, and when the fires went out, we'd hate ourselves."

"Sadie, I love you. Can't you believe that?"

She shook her head in disagreement. "But even if you did, Reese, I don't love you. Please forgive me for saying it so bluntly, but I have to be honest with you."

He exhaled slowly, as though he were trying to minimize the effects of some terrible blow to the abdomen. But the expression on his face never changed, and he continued to speak patiently to Sadie. "I don't believe you. You love me, Sadie. You just don't know it yet. And I'm willing to give you all the time you need until you finally figure it out for yourself."

Nervousness made her giggle. "You're awfully sure of yourself."

He lifted her hand to his lips and kissed it. "No, Sadie, I'm awfully sure of you."

She extracted her hand from his and stroked the rabbit. "There's something you have to understand about me, Reese. I have to be needed, or I can't be happy. Sniffles needs me. Jerry Don needed me. But you don't. You're self-sufficient. There's no place for me in your life."

"If that's what you think, you're more confused than I realized. I don't need you the way a little boy needs a mother, Sadie. I need you the way a man needs a woman." At last he kissed her, his mouth hungry for hers, his arms desperate to hold her close. He kissed her deeply and joyfully, giving of his strength and partaking of hers. And in that kiss he demonstrated what he could not explain in words: that strength was better than weakness, that maturity was better than adolescence, that giving and receiving were really the same thing—and that he knew her heart might someday be able to love again.

Chapter Fourteen

On Friday night, Reese met Sadie at the airport in Amarillo and drove her the fifty miles to Tascosa. He seemed aloof and had little to say until Sadie joshed him about his moodiness.

"Sorry, sweetheart. I'm trying hard not to say anything that will influence your decision, and that doesn't leave much to talk about." He kept his eyes on the highway, pointing to newly plowed fields ready for planting with winter wheat. "What did you do with Sniffles?" he asked.

"Vince is taking care of him for me this weekend."

Reese mumbled something unintelligible.

"Vince is my very good friend," Sadie said, amused at his reaction. "I honestly don't know what I'd have done without him." When he continued to grumble, she said, "Reese, it's okay for people to have friends of the opposite sex, you know. I don't fuss at you for being such good friends with Wynona, and you brag about her all the time. I'm surprised Tom doesn't get jealous of *you*."

"Why would he be jealous of me, for heaven's sake?"

"I can't imagine," Sadie said in a droll voice, ticking off Reese's assets. "It couldn't be your looks, or your money, or your dynamic personality. Not to mention your sex appeal."

Reese seemed embarrassed by her flattery. "Tom's got about as much money as I have. More irrigated land, less native grass and cattle."

"Are *you* jealous of *Tom*?" Sadie turned sideways on the seat so she could see his expression.

"Sometimes." He was unexpectedly brusque.

"But why, Reese?"

He shrugged, obviously not wanting to discuss the matter.

Sadie leaned over and laid her head on Reese's shoulder. "Sorry," she said. "I shouldn't have pried. I didn't know it still bothered you that Wynona married Tom instead of you."

He gave her a surprised look. "It doesn't," he said. "It never did. What I envy is his family—four healthy kids, a wife he loves, and a comfortable home."

Sadie wrinkled her brow in confusion. "But if you had married Wynona, you'd have a family of your own by now."

"Sure, but I'd rather have a family with you, Sadie—if you don't keep me waiting till we're too old." He ruffled her silky hair. "Sorry. I wasn't going to put any pressure on you."

"Reese, why didn't Wynona marry you?"

"Do you really want to know?" There was something guarded in his expression.

She nodded in assent.

"Then you're going to have to ask Wynona."

On Saturday Sadie dressed with extra care to make the right impression on her job interview. She wanted to project an image of maturity and authority so the school board would know she could handle a principal's responsibilities despite her youth. At twenty-eight, she would be younger than most of the teachers she would have to supervise, and when she wore jeans with her hair tied back, she didn't look any older than the students themselves. She'd debated about wearing a navy suit or a black A-line dress, and finally settled on a gray-and-white striped linen dress with a dove-gray jacket. The ensemble looked professional but not overly severe, and the gray toned down the red in her hair and the green in her eyes. She definitely didn't want to remind the board members of the young cheerleader she'd once been.

She added a final dab of lip gloss, patted her hair one last time and went into the living room. "How do I look?" she asked her mother and Al Peterson.

"Just lovely, dear."

"You don't look like any other principal that's ever been seen around here," Al said, chuckling. "They'll ask me why I didn't decide to retire a long time ago."

"Oh, dear," Sadie said, her brow furrowed. "Maybe I should've worn my navy suit, after all."

Al shrugged off her remark. "It's time for a change, Sadie. The school board will accept you just the way you are."

"I hope you're right. There are seven board members, counting Reese. I've got to have at least four votes, and he's going to abstain, because he says it would be a conflict of interest for him to vote for me. Mr. Carney already said he'll never vote for a woman principal, because she wouldn't be able to keep students disciplined."

"Don't you worry about Melvin Carney. I swear, the reason that man keeps getting reelected to the board is because they can always count on him to vote against everything. Folks in town think it would look bad if every vote went seven to zero. Looks better in the newspaper when the vote is reported six to one."

Sadie looked at her watch for the third time. It would take her exactly six minutes to drive to the school. She didn't want to be late, but it wouldn't be good to arrive too early, either. She was beginning to feel very nervous about this interview. She could almost be amused at herself. She didn't know whether she wanted the job or not, but she wanted them to offer it to her.

"Do you have any questions in mind to ask the board?" Al said. "They'll be expecting you to have some."

"Oh, yes, I have lots of questions. I want to know if they'll let me use part of the grant money to put a portable classroom in the fields where the migrants are working. I think more parents would let their children attend class that way. And I want to ask if they'll let me start a program for gifted children—" She gave them a sheepish smile. "Sorry. I guess I still sound like a cheerleader. I get excited when I think about all the things I'd like to try."

Al Peterson was pleased. "It takes lots of enthusiasm to be a good principal, Sadie. You've got to inspire the teachers as well as the students if you're going to be an effective leader. But you can't inspire anybody without enthusiasm, so you keep right on waving those pom-poms."

Sadie walked over to the sofa, where he sat beside her mother, and gave him a hug. "Thanks, Al." She drew a deep breath and blew her mother a kiss. "Time to go," she said, crossing her fingers. "Wish me luck."

Reese Chandler was conspicuously absent from the school-board meeting, but the other six members were already seated at the conference table when Sadie arrived. After offering Sadie a cup of coffee and some friendly conversation, the board members became very businesslike. They went over her entire résumé, commenting on her coaching experience in another school district and inquiring pointedly about her win-loss record. They asked what new programs she'd like to see implemented in Tascosa, and listened for more than an hour to her ideas about a portable classroom for migrant children and new courses for gifted and talented children.

Melvin Carney pursed his thin lips and peered at her over the top of his glasses. His gray hair, thinning on top, had been slicked back, and he wore a double-breasted brown suit that must have been twenty years old. "What do you think about the education reforms?"

Sadie might have known he'd be the one to ask the loaded question about the controversial new law. "The reforms are working," she said. "Student test scores are up significantly after only three years. There's more accountability for student perfor-mance, and good teachers are making more money now that we've got a career ladder that rewards out-standing performance."

She hesitated a moment. Feelings ran high on the controversial reform bill, and if three of the people sitting around the conference table disagreed with her, the principal's job would go to someone else.

Did she really *want* the job? She'd been telling her-self she didn't care one way or the other. A sudden wrenching in her gut told her she did want the position, and badly. Her old enthusiasm had come back since she'd been considering all the wonderful opportunities she'd have to develop educational programs. As principal, she could make a real contribution to the lives of the young people who lived in Tascosa. The thought of being with students again, and of sharing their vitality and hopes for the future, had given her a new zest for life. Whether things worked out with Reese or not, her life would be meaningful again if she could help guide the next generation toward fulfilling their potential.

The sudden realization of how much she wanted the job made her tremble. And she not only wanted it; she *needed* it. She had to be able to give of herself to others in order to be a whole and complete person.

She turned to Mr. Carney, who pursed his lips and tapped his pencil against the edge of the table, then began to scowl. Beside him, Mr. Fisher evaded her glance and looked down at the table. Two votes gone. Sadie looked at Mrs. Bartlett, whose son had flunked chemistry and been put off the team last year because of the no-pass, no-play rule included in the reform bill. Her lips were pursed tightly. Three votes gone. Dr. Weaver, who'd been a state champion himself in his high-school days, turned and looked out the window. Miss Simpson, whose brother was mayor of Tascosa, and Mr. Sayres, the town's only lawyer, wore blank expressions. The vote would be no better than four to two against her.

There was a general squirming around the table, and people began to cough and mutter to one another.

"Any further questions for Miss McClure?" asked Miss Simpson, this year's board president. "Well, then," she said, "I believe it's time for the board to go into executive session to discuss Miss McClure's application, together with those of the other candidates. We'll notify you of our decision as soon as possible." Miss Simpson tidied the stray hairs that had slipped loose from her bun. "I wish to say that I disagree with some of your views, Miss McClure. I believe very strongly that each student should develop whatever talents and capacities he has to the fullest. But we must keep in mind that we have a duty to our taxpayers, and some of the reforms are entirely too expensive—as well as unnecessary."

There was a general murmur of agreement from several of the others.

Sadie's cheeks reddened, but she said with sincerity, "I respect your right to a different opinion—just as I hope you respect mine." She stood to go. "Thank you very much for your time and interest."

Mr. Sayres, the lawyer, saw her to the door. "We'll send you a letter with our decision early next week."

"Thank you," Sadie said with a smile. She knew all too well that successful job applicants received telephone calls. Only losers got letters.

Sadie's mother and Al Peterson tried to cheer her up when she returned home, but they were pessimistic about her chances of receiving a job offer after she'd told them about her meeting with the school board. It seemed strange to Sadie that she could experience such a terrible sense of loss over a job that she hadn't even known she really wanted until halfway through the interview.

"You remembered to invite Reese for supper, didn't you, dear? He may have a better idea what the board will do." Nelda stood up and arranged one crutch under her arm, then started toward the kitchen.

Sadie nodded. "He's coming over about seven o'clock. He said he'd be busy at the ranch all afternoon." She wished now that he'd scheduled things differently so he could be here with her. It might help to talk things over with him. She sighed. What was she going to do with herself until seven o'clock? It was barely three now. "I'll help you get the food cooked for supper," she offered.

"That's all right, dear. Al and I will do it. We work at the same pace and don't get in each other's way."

"What are you cooking tonight, Nelda?" Al asked. "Besides those fluffy biscuits and cream gravy, I mean."

"I don't know. Let's see what we can find in the refrigerator."

Al followed Nelda into the kitchen, and Sadie could hear them laughing together as they explored the refrigerator and planned a menu. How quickly Al had become a fixture in her mother's life, Sadie thought. She actually seemed younger and healthier.

Sadie got up and prowled the living room, hunting for something to read. Finding nothing of interest, she turned on the TV set and decided she wasn't up for the roller-skating derby. She had to find something to do with herself or she'd be climbing the walls by seven o'clock.

She felt tears filling her eyes. But she was absolutely determined not to start crying *now*. It would upset her mother, and it just wouldn't do. She got up, trying to think of something constructive that would get her mind off the interview. The whole house was immaculate, supper was under control, the ripe vegetables had already been picked from the garden....

She wandered into her bedroom to take off her linen dress and change into a comfortable pair of cotton shorts and a halter top. Every time she walked into the room she was bombarded with purple-and-white ruffles and high-school souvenirs. She decided it was time to pack all that stuff away in the attic, where it belonged. Surely her mother had another bedspread somewhere.

She went out to the garage and found some empty cardboard boxes, then carried them back to her bedroom and began to fold the ruffled curtains and bedspread. She took one of the small boxes and used it for the photographs on the bulletin board. These brought up memories better kept out of sight, though her fingers lingered on each picture before she gently stowed it away. What wonderful dreams we had then, she thought, but they slipped through our fingers because we were too young and didn't know how to hold on to them. Would time give them another chance, another set of dreams? She thought of Reese and smiled. Someday, maybe...

She opened and closed the dresser drawers. Most of them were empty, but some held mementos from high school and college. She sat cross-legged in the middle of the stripped bed and sorted through a long-forgotten bundle of photographs. These were really old, going back to junior high and elementary school. She found a picture of the whole first-grade class with Miss Cope, her favorite teacher of all. There in the back row was Reese, and here was Sadie, kneeling in front. Wynona was kneeling beside her, and on the far left was Jerry Don. Sadie brought the photograph closer to her eyes, studying it carefully. What round, baby faces they'd had then, without the angles and planes hammered out by maturity. What sweet, beautiful, innocent, childish faces.

Sadie laid the photograph on the bed and buried her face in her hands. How long had that picture been there, lying in wait for this very moment to break her heart with the truth it had hidden away? Trembling like an old, old woman, Sadie walked down the hallway to her mother's bedroom and reached for the telephone.

"Wynona?" she said when her best friend answered. "Can you come over right away? I need to talk to you. I'll be down at the cottonwood grove, on the tree swing."

"What's wrong, Sadie? You sound terrible. Did something happen at the interview?"

"The interview? It was a disaster."

"Tom's mother and sister are here, and they can watch the children for me. I'll be right over."

Sadie slipped out the side door and made her way to the tree swing. She hadn't been there long when she heard the slam of a car door and footsteps running through the yard.

"Sadie, hon, I'm so sorry," Wynona said, kneeling beside the swing and putting her arms around Sadie.

Sadie buried her face on Wynona's shoulder, feeling the crisp, springy blond curls against her cheek. The twins had those same springy curls, and the baby.

"Go ahead and cry, hon," Wynona crooned, reaching in her pocket for a tissue to wipe the tears that trickled down Sadie's cheeks.

Sadie took the tissue and sat upright again. Her eyes never left Wynona's face, and she continued to weep soundlessly.

"What happened, hon? Tell me all about it," Wynona urged.

For an answer, Sadie reached under her hips, where she'd tucked away the first-grade class photograph. "There we are," she said. "All four of us."

Wynona reached for the photograph, a startled expression on her face. "Oh," she said. It was more an explosion of air than a word. Her fair skin turned crimson from the vee of her blouse to the roots of her hair. "I don't remember seeing this picture before," she said softly. Her finger stroked the image of Jerry Don, there on the left end, his silky blond hair brushed straight and smooth, his blue eyes glinting mischief. "Aaron looks just like him, doesn't he?"

Sadie hiccupped, trying to choke back her tears. "All these years I've been bitter because Jerry Don's death cheated me out of having children with him. This is the son I imagined we'd have." She buried her face in her hands and turned away from Wynona. "Why, Wynona? You had Reese. Why did you take Jerry Don away from me?"

Wynona began to cry softly. "I didn't, Sadie. The last time I ever saw Jerry Don, the morning he got killed, he was still saying he wanted to marry you."

Sadie looked at her in surprise. "Did he know you were pregnant?"

Wynona nodded. "I had to tell him. He kept saying we'd work it out. He said he'd marry me as soon as school was out."

"That sounds like Jerry Don," Sadie said harshly. "He probably thought he could dream up some way to marry both of us."

Wynona reached for Sadie's hand. "I really loved him, Sadie. Sometimes I wish I hadn't, but I did. I've never regretted having Aaron, because he's all that's left of Jerry Don."

"Is that any excuse for what you did to me? You were my best friend, Wynona, and you betrayed me! Because of you, Jerry Don betrayed me! And all these years I've been through hell because I felt so guilty about what *I'd* done to *him*." A hysterical giggle burst from her throat.

"Sometimes I wonder what would have happened if he hadn't gotten killed," Wynona said, lowering herself to sit cross-legged on the grass. Sadie got off the swing and sat down beside her. Anger and pain flowed between the two of them, but their hands were gripped together as tightly as when they'd walked in the dark as children.

"I hated you then," Wynona continued. "I thought Jerry Don loved *me*, but you were the homecoming queen and you know how he was. He needed all that popularity to keep his ego pumped up. I was a home-town girl who clerked at the grocery store. I couldn't compete with a college beauty queen like you, hon, not in Jerry Don's eyes. So he sneaked home to see me every chance he got, but he wouldn't give up the idea of marrying you."

"It must have been awful for you."

Wynona shrugged. "I loved him. I was willing to take whatever he had to give. The worst part was getting those letters from you every week, telling me all about your wedding plans." She lifted stricken eyes to Sadie. "I felt terrible about that. I knew what I was doing would hurt you, but I couldn't help myself."

"Did Reese know?"

Wynona nodded. "Jerry Don told him. I guess he had to talk to somebody."

"I'm sure it nearly killed Reese. He loved you, Wynona, and you betrayed him, too."

"No," Wynona protested, shaking her head. She gave Sadie's hand a fierce shake. "I had a terrible crush on Reese when we were sophomores, but he never had eyes for anybody but you. Sometimes I think he loved you from the first time he ever laid eyes on you, that day we started kindergarten." She reached for the picture and studied Reese's face. "See? He's looking at you from four rows away."

"Don't be ridiculous," Sadie said sharply, but she took the picture and looked for herself. "I think he's looking at you."

Wynona wiped away her tears with one hand, leaving a streak of mascara across her cheek. "Reese is a wonderful guy, Sadie."

"Well, sure. He was always my best friend. I couldn't always count on Jerry Don, but Reese was there when I needed him. He never let me down, not once. But, oh, how we fought!"

"Those years were hell for Reese, Sadie. He loved you, and he loved Jerry Don, too. He was too decent to betray his best friend, so he kept his mouth shut and ate his heart out." A new tear trickled down her cheek. "We were so young and foolish," she whispered. "None of us knew how to handle what was happening to us, and we botched up everything. We need to thank the good Lord for giving us another chance."

"Jerry Don didn't get another chance."

"No, but he left me with Aaron."

Sadie stared up into the bright blue sky. "Why didn't you marry Reese, Wynona? I always wondered about that. I know he asked you, and when you married Tom instead, he went off to Chicago and married that girl up there on the rebound."

"Did you ever see her picture? She looked a whole lot like you, hon. Reese was on the rebound, all right, but it was because you'd gone away and wouldn't come back. He was looking for a substitute for *you*, not for me."

"Reese didn't ask *me* to marry him, Wynona. He asked you." A long-buried resentment surfaced. Sadie had felt completely abandoned when she learned Reese had proposed marriage to Wynona the day following Jerry Don's death. She now realized that her anger had caused a rift in her relationship with Wynona. That was why she'd never wanted to discuss Reese and Jerry Don with her best girlfriend.

"He asked me to marry him because he loved Jerry Don, Sadie. The last thing he would ever be able to do for Jerry Don was give his unborn child a name."

The information surprised Sadie, yet it all fit together. Reese was incredibly loyal to the people he loved. "Then why didn't you marry him?" she asked.

Wynona didn't answer for a while, trying to find words for something too painful to communicate. "I was crushed when we got the news about Jerry Don's death," she said at last. "I thought it was my punishment for what I'd done. I wanted to try to make things right somehow, or at least as right as I could. I knew I had to get married, but it wouldn't have been fair to Reese when I knew he loved *you*. There was no sense messing up another person's life, too. Tom Evans was older than we were, but I knew he sort of had a crush on me. I told him about the baby coming, and he said he'd marry me. Just like that. And do you know what? He loves Aaron just as much as he does Biff and Becka and Melanie. I didn't love Tom when I married him, but he was so good to me and loved me so much that I came to love him more than I ever dreamed it was possible to love someone.''

"More than you loved Jerry Don?''

"Compared to my love for Tom, what I felt for Jerry Don was puppy love. It was all physical.''

"Yeah, I know about that kind. That's what Reese and I have for each other.''

"Sadie McClure! You're the biggest fool I've ever met, if you believe that!'' Wynona squeezed Sadie's hand. "When are you going to wake up and realize that you've been in love with Reese for years, just like he's been in love with you? You're both so scared to admit it that you try to keep the whole state of Texas in between you. It's a mystery to me why you keep wasting these good years when you could be loving and making babies together.''

Sadie lay back on the grass and sighed. She was beginning to feel a new sense of peace. The past, with all its mistakes, was finished. She didn't have to keep looking back to the girl she'd been. The truth had set her free. Now she could focus on the future and become the woman she wanted to be.

"Wynona, do you happen to know where Reese is working this afternoon? I want to go see him."

Wynona got to her feet and offered Sadie a hand. "He's down by the creek. You'll need to take Al's four-wheel drive to get there." There was something mysterious in the smile Wynona gave Sadie. "Reese has a surprise for you, hon."

In Al Peterson's four-wheel-drive pickup truck, Sadie retraced the trail she'd ridden on horseback with Reese and his cowboys a few weeks earlier. The truck stirred up a heavy column of dust, and even with the windows rolled up, dust sifted in and filled her eyes and nose. When she reached the place where she and Reese had built the fire for their picnic, she saw that a bulldozer had recently been there and cut a road. He must want to make the site more accessible, she thought, and wondered why. She pulled the truck onto the new road and followed it to its end. Ahead of her, sheltered in a grove of tall cottonwoods and elms, a concrete slab had been poured and wood framing started for a building.

She got out of the truck and heard the sound of hammering. Reese must be here somewhere, because his pickup was parked near some junipers. Sadie reached into Al's pickup and blared the horn three times.

"Reese!" she cried. "Where are you?"

He came around the side of the framework, wearing only his jeans and cowboy boots. His bare chest and shoulders were covered with sweat, and beads of perspiration trickled down his forehead. "Sadie!" he called, waving at her as he came running to meet her. He lifted her into his arms and swung her around. "Sadie, Sadie," he said, pulling her face to his and kissing her hungrily. "How did you know where to find me?"

"Wynona told me." Sadie slipped her arms around Reese's neck and lifted herself on tiptoe to kiss him again. "I love kissing you," she whispered, brushing tiny kisses against his lips and chin. "Wynona told me everything," she said, burying her face in his neck.

He tilted her head back enough so that he could see her face. "So now you know. Are you okay?"

"It hurt at first. I wish she'd told me a long time ago."

Reese shook his head. "You weren't ready to hear it, Sadie. You had to work through your own grief for Jerry Don before you could take on Wynona's."

"But think of all the time I've wasted," she said. "When we could have been together."

Reese kissed her tenderly on the lips, then buried his hands in her hair. "Sometimes I got impatient, but I knew there wouldn't be room in your heart for me until you finally got rid of Jerry Don's ghost."

Sadie snuggled against his bare chest and ran her fingers up and down his spine. "You have a nice spine," she said. "It's not bony at all."

Reese smiled, shaking his head at such an incongruous remark. "How did your interview turn out?" he asked.

Sadie frowned at the reminder. "I'd forgotten all about it," she admitted. "It was awful, Reese. They're not going to offer me a job, because I told them I supported the education reforms."

He laughed aloud. "That must have gone over with a bang. Did Miss Simpson tell you about the board's need to protect the taxpayers from all those unnecessary frills?"

"How did you know?"

"I've heard her make that speech before. You're not the only applicant who spoke in favor of the reforms."

"I'm not?"

"You're probably the only former coach who did, though."

"Well, I decided I was going to tell them the truth. I don't want the job if I'm going to have to tell people what they want to hear, instead of what I think is right."

Reese squeezed her in a hug so tight she could scarcely breathe. "Good for you."

She ran her fingers up his cheek and into his dark hair. "I believe you mean that," she said.

"Of course I do."

"But it means I won't get the job, Reese. I need a job if I'm going to come back to Tascosa."

"*If* you come back to Tascosa?"

She was flustered. "Well, I suppose I'll come back anyway."

There was a mischievous gleam in his eye. "You're damned right you'll come back anyway."

"But, Reese, I have to have a job. I can't move in with Mom and expect her to support me."

"Your mother wouldn't have you back on a bet. She's too busy living her own life to mess with you." He put his arms around her waist and pulled her close against him. Her halter top left her midriff and back almost completely bare, and he began to move his hands sensuously across her shoulder blades and down to her waist. "I don't know what's going to become of you, Sadie, now that you've blown the only available job in Tascosa and your own mother won't have you." He moved his mouth against her throat and up to her ear. "Maybe somebody will take pity on you and bring you in off the street. Or bully the school board into hiring you anyway. For a small price, I might be able to persuade them to take a chance on you." He kissed her eyelids and nose, then nipped her chin gently.

"Kiss me, Reese, and make me forget my problems," she said, offering her lips.

He groaned and kissed her deeply in a frantic fusion of lips and tongues. When they drew apart, they were breathless with desire and wonder.

"Come let me show you what I'm working on," Reese said, taking her hand and leading her toward the framed structure. "You'll have to use your imagination and visualize the way it's going to look when it's finished." A rough set of steps had been placed at the front of the structure to allow entry. "These are temporary," he said. He pointed to a joist above their heads. "That's where your porch swing will hang," he said. "Do you think this veranda is big enough to suit you?"

Sadie looked at him in bewilderment. "What is this, Reese?"

"This is the dream house I'm building for my bride. It's going to have everything you ever told me you wanted—a big front porch with a swing—" he led her inside "—a native stone fireplace with a raised hearth," he said, pointing to the corner where there was nothing but a chimney pipe going up through the roof framework. "Let's go around to the back. That's the best part. It's our bedroom. Like it so far?"

She was so overcome she couldn't speak. "Reese, when did you start building this house?"

"The day after we made love here by the creek. The day you left Tascosa."

"But, Reese, I told you I was never coming back."

He tilted her face to his and brushed her lips. "I didn't believe you. That day I knew it was only a matter of time until you came back and married me."

"How could you know that, when I didn't even know it myself?"

"Don't you remember the day at the creek, Sadie, and that night at the fire station?"

She blushed. "How could I forget? But it didn't necessarily mean I'd come back."

"Didn't it? When you finally gave yourself to me, you gave me your heart, too. It just took a while for you to realize it."

"How did you know?"

Their eyes met. "I can't explain it. I knew it in here." Reese pointed to his heart. "Maybe it was the sweetness between us. I knew you were mine and I'd never give you up." They exchanged a lingering kiss. "Come let me show you the rest of the house before you get me so distracted I forget what I'm doing."

They walked to the back of the house, where large spaces had been left in the framing for glass panes. The room was open on three sides, with the canyon and creek to the south and prairie fields to the east and west.

"Remember when we were young and you talked about wanting a bedroom where you could see the sunrise in the morning and the sunset in the evening? I was here early this morning, and you can't believe how incredible the view is when the sun comes up, all pink and gold."

"What are these other rooms?" Sadie asked, pointing.

"This one next to our bedroom is the nursery. These other two bedrooms are for when the kids are older." He took her hand and led her through the framed-off spaces. "Here's your kitchen, with a place for a bricked-in oven and another fireplace where you can rock the baby." He pulled Sadie into his arms. "This is our home, Sadie—yours and mine—if you'll have me.''

Sadie buried her head against Reese's bare chest. What a wonderful man she'd fallen in love with. Joy rose within her and spilled over. She clung to him, her eyes bright with tears. ''Reese—''

''Yes, sweetheart,'' he said, searching for her lips.

''I love you, Reese.''

He gently touched her lips with his finger, and his own eyes were bright with unshed tears.

''Reese, do you love me?''

''Don't you know I do?''

''Yes, but I need to hear you say it.''

''In that case—'' Reese wrapped her in a bear hug so tight she could scarcely breathe. ''In that case, Sadie McClure, let me be the first to tell you that there's never been a day in my life when I haven't been in love with you. I loved you before you lost your baby teeth, before you learned to read and write, before you filled out and got breasts—'' he moved his hands upward as he continued. ''I loved you long before Jerry Don even knew you existed. I love you this minute, I'll love you as long as I have breath, and God willing, I'll love you for all eternity. There's never been a time in my life when I had a soul of my own, because it's always been a part of yours. There's no *me*, Sadie; there's only *us*. I love you so much that I have no life apart from you, and the last few years without you have been a hell on earth. I love you so much that—''

But after all, Reese Chandler was a man of few words. He stopped talking and demonstrated his love, to Sadie's delight and total satisfaction.

* * * * *

Silhouette Special Edition

**MORE SPECIAL THAN EVER,
SAY THESE TOP AUTHORS:**

JO ANN ALGERMISSEN

"To me, writing—or reading—a Silhouette Special Edition *is* special. Longer, deeper, more emotionally involving than many romances, 'Specials' allow me to climb inside the hearts of my characters. I personally struggle with each of their problems, sympathize with the heroine, and almost fall in love with the hero myself! What I truly enjoy is knowing that the commitment between the hero and heroine will be as lasting as my own marriage—forever. That's special."

TRACY SINCLAIR

"I hope everyone enjoys reading Silhouette Special Editions as much as I enjoy writing them. The world of romance is a magic place where dreams come true. I love to travel to glamorous locales with my characters and share in the excitement that fills their lives. These people become real to me. I laugh and cry with them; I rejoice in their ultimate happiness. I am also reluctant to see the adventure end because I am having such a good time. That's what makes these books so special to me—and, I hope, to you."

SSE-A2

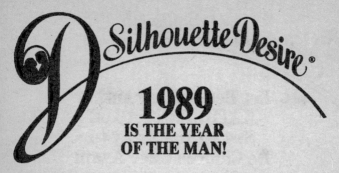

Silhouette Desire®

1989
IS THE YEAR
OF THE MAN!

What makes a romance? A special man, of course, and Silhouette Desire celebrates that fact with *twelve* of them! From Mr. January to Mr. December, every month has a tribute to the Silhouette Desire hero—our **MAN OF THE MONTH!**

Sexy, macho, charming, irritating . . . irresistible! Nothing can stop these men from sweeping you away. Created by some of your favorite authors, each man is custom-made for pleasure—*reading* pleasure—so don't miss a single one.

Mr. January is Blake Donavan in RELUCTANT FATHER by Diana Palmer
Mr. February is Hank Branson in THE GENTLEMAN INSISTS by Joan Hohl
Mr. March is Carson Tanner in NIGHT OF THE HUNTER by Jennifer Greene
Mr. April is Slater McCall in A DANGEROUS KIND OF MAN by Naomi Horton
Mr. May is Luke Harmon in VENGEANCE IS MINE by Lucy Gordon
Mr. June is Quinn McNamara in IRRESISTIBLE by Annette Broadrick

And that's only the half of it—
so get out there and find your man!

Silhouette Desire's

MAN OF THE MONTH . . .

MOM-1

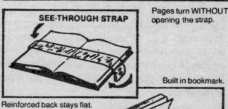

COMING IN APRIL

NAVY BLUES
Debbie Macomber

Between the devil and the deep blue sea . . .

At Christmastime, Lieutenant Commander Steve Kyle finds his heart
anchored by the past, so he vows to give his ex-wife wide berth. But
Carol Kyle is quaffing milk and knitting tiny pastel blankets with a
vengeance. She's determined to have a baby, and only one man will
do as father-to-be—the only man she's ever loved . . . her own
bullheaded ex-husband! Can the wall of bitterness protecting Steve's
battered heart possibly withstand the hurricane force of his Navy
wife's will?

You met Steve and Carol in NAVY WIFE (Special Edition #494)—
you'll cheer for them in NAVY BLUES (Special Edition #518). (And
as a bonus for NAVY WIFE fans, newlyweds Rush and Lindy Cal-
laghan reveal a surprise of their own. . . .)

Each book stands alone—together they're Debbie Macomber's most
delightful duo to date! Don't miss

NAVY BLUES
Available in April,
only in *Silhouette Special Edition*.
Having the "blues" was never
so much fun!

SE518-1